Amrach and the Paraclete

Amrach and the Paraclete

John Glass

Authentic
LIFESTYLE

First published in 2004 by Authentic Lifestyle
Reprinted 2004
10 09 08 07 06 05 04   7 6 5 4 3 2

Authentic Lifestyle is an imprint of Authentic Media,
PO Box 300, Carlisle, Cumbria CA3 0QS, UK
Box 1047, Waynesboro, GA 30830-2047, USA
www.paternoster-publishing.com

British Library Cataloguing in Publication Data

A catalogue record for this book is available from the British
Library

ISBN 1-85078-556-2

Cover design by Pete Barnsley
Print Management by Adare Carwin
Printed and bound by AIT Nørhaven A/S, Denmark

Contents

1

The Remnant Legend

You could roam the galaxies for centuries and never find the land of Phos. Such worlds do not lie within the realms of time and space. Yet it is real. It is so real that without it nothing else in the universe would have meaning.

The land once extended far further than the territory it presently occupies. Once, it covered the entire land mass; but that was before the Great Rebellion which took place long before anyone could remember. Phos lay to the East and what became known as The Dominion of Harag lay to the west. Separating these two centres of power were the Plains of Shephelah: a wild and barren expanse that, as it could not support life, was entirely devoid of population.

The area in the west was now ruled by an army of demonic warriors called the Princes of Harag who brutally suppressed the provinces under their control.

The circumstances that caused the division within the land were hidden in the mists of history. People spoke of the Rebellion but little more was known. All the sacred parchments which chronicled the truth of the matter had been destroyed and the telling of sagas and tales that related to the incident had long been punishable by death.

The Princes, knowing the power of storytelling, had circulated many contradictory accounts in order to confuse the population. Yet there were some that possessed a collection of scrolls that over the passing of time were known as the Remnant Legend – documents that had been gleaned from ancient fragments of the original parchments and now committed to memory.

The Princes of Harag knew of the existence of the scrolls that comprised the Remnant Legend but, despite all their efforts, had never been able to discover their location. Nevertheless there was no account of the Rebellion, even in the Legend. What it did record, however, were the exploits of the wise and mighty ruler of the land of Phos – he who had taken upon himself the appearance of a great lion.

Throughout Harag small gatherings would take place where men, women and children came to discuss the Remnant Legend with those who were courageous enough to teach its truths.

On the day that was to begin the chain of events that would change the destiny of multitudes, the sun rose just as it always had, the birds sang as they always did and Amrach's two sons said farewell to their father as he set off for the woods. They knew that their mother would enter the woods at a different access point some time later. Taking a different route, the boys would then follow when further time had elapsed.

It was only when he knew that he was absolutely safe that Amrach began the routine that had now become familiar to him. There were eleven men and women with whom he would be meeting within the hour – all of them teachers of the legend. They were never told the area where they would congregate in case any of them fell into the hands of one of the Dominion of Harag's spies. They knew only to make their way to a place where a trail would begin and then, by signs left by Amrach with sticks and stones, all would eventually arrive safely at their destination.

When everyone had assembled it was Amrach's wife who was the first to address the group. The small knot of people sought out places to sit in the clearing. Some chose a fallen tree, while others sat astride some of the large wicker baskets that they had brought with them.

'It's so wonderful to see you all again,' she began gently. 'In just a few hours many of our friends will find their way to the trail that my husband has set and they will be joining us here. We know that all will be as eager as ever and open to be taught. We must spend our time profitably before they come. Our time is precious. It is vital that we relate the Legend accurately and simply.'

And so, just as Amrach's wife had said, the group made their preparations. Those who were the main speakers communicated in hushed voices and those who had carried the provisions set about unpacking food and drink from the baskets.

A crack of twigs caused the group momentarily to freeze. But their alarm subsided as soon as they noticed Amrach's two boys emerging stealthily from the bushes. They were the first of the scores of folk who would assemble on that fateful day.

It was always the same on such occasions. Once the stories began about the valiant deeds of the Lion, time flew by. As dusk fell a few lamps were lit but their number was kept to the barest minimum. Before long it would be necessary to bring the proceedings to a close; but this was never done until time had been set aside for questions.

There were several children in the group. Every one of them was as enthusiastic as their parents to learn and every bit as courageous as the bravest adults. No one, young or old, would put themselves at such risk of discovery were they not devoted to the teaching of the Remnant Legend. Though none had ever seen the Lion, and never thought themselves likely to, they had developed a great affection for him – as well as a respectful sense of awe.

It was one of the youngest members of the crowd who asked the final question of the day.

'Why do we always call it the Remnant Legend? What does "remnant" mean?'

'A remnant means "the small part that is left over",' answered Amrach's wife.

No one ever minded asking her a question even though they might be the only one who did not know the answer. She was always patient and never moved on to another enquiry until she was absolutely sure that she was fully understood. The children loved her.

'You see,' she continued, 'there are very many people who live in our land but only a tiny number know about the Legend and all of those are in this wood right now. Some people think that something can only be true if most of the people believe it. But we know that the way of the Lion is the best path to follow even if we are the only ones who are aware of it.'

Before she could continue further there came the most terrifying and chilling shrieks from the bushes around them. No sentries had been posted as everyone had wanted to listen to the Legend. In consequence, no one was aware that, while all ears were tuned to the speakers, warriors sent by the Princes of Harag had not only discovered them, but completely surrounded them.

The men fell upon the group with clubs, swords and horrifying shouts.

Everything was in confusion as people ran in all directions. The cordon that had been placed around the clearing was totally firm. It was impossible for anyone to escape. Amrach took a blow to his head and fell like a stone. Four of the warriors rushed towards the boys who, unarmed like everyone else, stood close to their mother in a futile gesture of protection.

'These growing lads will make fine slaves for sure,' one of the warriors snarled.

'No!' cried their mother as she, in her turn, attempted to shield them. Ruthlessly they knocked her to the ground and she fell heavily against a large stone. Instantly, she was dead.

Her sons called out to her and struggled violently, but they were vastly overwhelmed by the numbers, size and ferocity of their captors.

* * * * * *

Dawn broke over the wood. The birdsong and a gentle breeze that began to rustle the leaves around the clearing were the only witnesses to the dreadful reality of the previous night.

Amrach twitched and stirred. He tried to get to his feet but fell back. His vision blurred, he reached out towards an oblong shape that he concluded must be a rock but as he did so the overturned wicker basket gave way and he dropped once again to the ground.

At the same moment that strength rallied in his legs, frightening thoughts raced to his mind. Stumbling through what looked like a battlefield he came to the lifeless body of his wife and, overwhelmed by grief, collapsed yet again to his knees sobbing.

He hardly had time to begin to give vent to his pain before he considered the fate of his boys. He moved around from one fallen friend to another. He knew them all well. He thought, as he searched, of the many times had he waited until all had safely assembled before commencing the meetings that centred around the Legend. All were accounted for – except his sons.

*   *   *   *   *   *

Several days passed before Amrach was able to bury those who had been killed. The Princes of Harag had assumed that there had been no survivors beyond the two slaves that had been taken. Now, were he to bring anyone else into his confidence, not only would he have supplied intelligence that he was alive, but he would also reveal that he was a member of the Remnant. Even if his neighbours did not betray him it would not be too long before Harag's spies would learn of his existence.

Amrach could not stay in the Dominion of Harag but, at the same time, there was nowhere else for him to go. Phos, the land of which the Legend spoke, was a very long distance across the plains. There had been stories of individuals who had tried for a multitude of reasons to flee Harag, but none had survived. Those who had travelled the edges of Shephelah had come across the skeletal remains and every discovery had underlined the futility of the attempt. The only ones who could gather the necessary supplies to move people to the land, had they so wished, were the demonic rulers of Harag themselves. Rumour had it they had used such resources to transfer some of their spies into the outskirts of Phos. But no one was able to verify whether such a story was true or fiction.

With the death of Amrach's wife and friends and the enslavement of his sons, the grip that the Princes of Harag had over the Dominion was total. Furthermore, he was now the only person alive who knew of the Remnant Legend.

It was now clear to him that, whatever the cost, he had to try to flee Harag. But Amrach was motivated by far more than simply a desire to escape. Though only a short while ago the idea would have seemed totally preposterous, he had decided to seek an audience with the Lion himself! Having thought it, he now felt the need to speak the statement out. Each time the level of his declaration became louder until the ravens in the many tall trees around his house were frightened into flight. His time of whisperings, he concluded, was over.

When he eventually set out he took with him his horse and a string of three mules. The wicker baskets which he had retrieved from the wood were filled again with food and drink. While the supplies looked as if they were sufficient for a small army, Amrach was well aware that they would only last him for a few weeks and that the demands of the journey were bound to overtake even these resources.

* * * * * *

In the weeks that followed, although he ate and drank sparingly, his rations were soon diminished. One by one the baskets were discarded. Each of the mules, their burden having been reduced to nothing and now no longer needed, were released. He knew that they could find their way back and survive on what sparse vegetation there was within the barren wilderness that for too long had been his home.

All his supplies having been exhausted, Amrach tilted back his head and finished the last remaining drops from his water bottle. He knew that unless he reached his destination within the next few days the Princes of Harag would have defeated him before his quest had even begun.

2

The Stronghold of Theotes

Few horsemen are found riding the Plains of Shephelah in the hours before dawn. The damp night mists that hang over the marshes and loiter over the lower watery expanses of that region make travelling treacherous even for those familiar with its barren terrain, but for others it is perilous beyond imagination.

Amrach's body, slumped forward in the saddle, lay semi-conscious along the horse's neck as his mount picked its stumbling way across stone-studded streams and into the darkness. False-footed for the final time, the animal staggered uncontrollably. It lurched backwards and, piercing the night air with a shrill cry, threw Amrach from its back as it collapsed to the ground. Its neck was broken.

When he stirred many hours later it was not to the feel of sodden earth and the smell of dead flesh, but rather to the caress of crisp white sheets and the fragrance of fresh flowers.

'Where—?' Amrach began.

'Enough, enough for now,' responded a voice which to Amrach seemed close but which he could not place in a room that swirled before him each time he tried to open his eyes.

'Rest more if you can,' the voice continued. 'There will be time enough for talking . . . '

What came next tailed off into silence as Amrach sank into a deep and therapeutic slumber.

How long he slept he did not know, but, when he awoke this time he was able at least to take in something of his surroundings. His head thumped painfully and it seemed that every inch of his body throbbed and ached.

The room was sparse and empty of all but the most basic of furnishings. Beside his bed, and over against a stone wall, was a wooden table upon which stood a water basin. The window through which sunlight streamed must, he concluded, be opened onto a garden for it was from that direction that the sweet-scented aroma travelled.

The bed creaked as Amrach attempted to raise his body to a sitting position. As if responding to a cue, the door opened and through it came a man who, even before he spoke, Amrach assumed owned the voice he had earlier heard. The 'voice' was followed closely by a young woman whom Amrach presumed to be his wife.

'Feeling better are we? You were in a dreadful state when we found you.'

It was not until this point that Amrach realised that his clothes were gone and that he was wearing a cream-coloured bed gown.

'My name is Darak and this is my wife. Do you feel well enough to eat yet?'

'Yes, yes thank you. How long—? My horse—? It's really very kind of you—Where—?'

'It's all right; everything has been taken care of. I am afraid that the horse is dead and we took the liberty of burying it. If someone had not been travelling on the edges of the Plains of Shephelah, I am sorry to say that you would have been dead too. But everything has been taken taken care of for the moment.'

'Darak, did you say?'

'Yes.'

'Darak, I don't know how to thank you. The truth is that I owe you my very life. I assure you that I will not prevail upon your hospitality any more. You have done enough for me already. If I could have my clothes—?'

'There is no question of you leaving here for a while, my friend. We have provisions enough for all of us. Our cottage may be humble but we have more than sufficient to meet our needs; and yours as well while you are here. You create no burden or imposition upon us at all. Anyway, you must tell us more about yourself. What's your name? Where are you from and, most of all, what on earth possessed you to go riding on the Plains of Shephelah in the middle of the night?'

Darak's wife, having seen that the stranger was awake and comparatively well, had left the room to prepare some food. She now returned with piping hot oatmeal gruel which, having thanked her for it, Amrach ate with great relish.

'My name is Amrach and I have travelled from what is now known as the Dominion of Harag.'

At this, the colour drained from the face of Darak's wife. She gasped and wondered who the stranger was that they had brought into their home and what would become of them because of it.

'It's all right,' said Amrach. 'Don't worry; I'm not of the bloodline of Harag myself. In fact the wretched condition in which you found me is a direct consequence of my encounter with his warriors. If I could continue . . .'

The young woman's face was still taut with anxiety yet she was obviously relieved to know that she and her husband were not in the danger that she had assumed a few moments previously. Darak, with some urgency, bade Amrach go on.

'Until a few months ago, Darak, I too had a wife, a family and fields from which we made our living. I had hoped to live long there. I had dreams that my wife and I would see our sons take over the lands, reap the crops and raise their own children in years to come. It is true that we did hear rumours that the Princes of Harag were marshalling their armies, but we never really thought that we would be their targets. The farmlands around us are verdant but there are few rich folks in our territory. We concluded that the spoil they might take from us would not be worth the bother of taking. Of course we know now that they were not just concerned with wealth but with conquest, dominion, capturing our land and taking our people – what was left of them – into slavery.'

Amrach felt it unwise to speak of the Remnant Legend. His hosts were kind but it would be some time before he would feel himself able to trust anyone enough to convey such information.

'There was no point in building fortresses or training armies,' he continued. 'Our people would have been no match for them anyway and our towers would not have withstood their battering rams. I was powerless to stop my wife being slain and I was helpless as my sons were being captured. It was only after I had been left for dead that I was eventually able to make my escape. The rest you know about.'

Darak's countenance expressed his sympathy. He had heard many stories about the Dominion of Harag but, until now, no survivors had ever crossed his path to confirm or deny the accounts that had been conveyed. Yet many stories there were and they never got less terrible by the telling.

'What made you travel in this direction?' Darak enquired.

'To gain an audience with the Lion at the Stronghold of Theotes,' replied Amrach. 'There is no other way forward now. The Princes of Harag, having consolidated their hold over my land, will stop at nothing in an attempt to bring their forces across the Plains of Shephelah to the very gates of Theotes itself. Only the Lion has the power to resist them.'

'And you know about the castle of Theotes, the residence of the Lion?' Darak tested him.

Amrach tensed noticeably. A severe head wound received weeks earlier combined with a tortuous ride across Shephelah had clearly blunted his guard. He must remember to be far more careful in future. He chose not to answer in the hope that he would not be pressed further.

'Darak, a straight answer if you will. What is the likelihood of the Lion granting me a hearing?'

Darak paused. He well knew that his new friend would not easily comprehend his reply, strangers seldom did. Only those who had come into contact with the Lion and his Commanders personally could ever really understand. He crossed the room to sit at the end of Amrach's bed, as if shortening the distance between them was going to make the communication more comprehensible.

'It's both the easiest and the hardest thing in the world,' offered Darak. 'It is the easiest in that no Being in the universe is more approachable, has more love, is more gentle or is more mighty.'

'Then how can it be difficult?' asked Amrach quizzically.

'Because . . .' And here Darak took a deep sigh, 'Because no one ever leaves the presence of the Lion the same as they go in. Everyone who meets him leaves his presence transformed and everything he touches increases in value. You see, Amrach, before anyone leaves the Stronghold he puts into their hand a Silver Sceptre. This sceptre is not just a memento of your encounter with him, neither is it a parting gift. It is a token of introduction that carries with it great responsibility. It is better never to have met the Lion at all than to meet him, receive the Silver Sceptre, and then later to lay it down.'

Amrach shifted his aching body on the bed, looking both for a more comfortable position and some suitable response.

'I hear what you are saying, good Darak, but I want to meet him just the same. Is it possible for you to arrange it?'

'Are you really sure? Take time to think the matter through.'

'I have had time enough to think on my journey here, and now there is little time to lose. I am sure that in a matter of weeks the Princes of Harag will begin to cross the Plains of Shephelah. You must arrange an audience. You have to make it possible.'

'Very well then,' said Darak. 'Be it as you wish. Tomorrow, if you are well enough, we shall set off on our journey to the Stronghold.'

Amrach slept well that night. He knew what it was to toss and turn fitfully when his mind was full. But the very thought of the magnitude of what lay before him took him far beyond the threshold of normal worry or natural care. However, when morning broke he was pleasantly surprised to find how easy it was to wash and dress, given his earlier ordeal.

Darak's wife prepared a hearty breakfast for them both and, as he made his way to the table, he noticed that provisions for the journey were already packed and lying on a chair by the door.

It was only when he stepped outside into the lane that he got a better perspective of the home that had become his sanctuary. It was typical of many of the simple dwelling places that made up the villages and hamlets of that area: well built, functional, yet comfortable. He had known for some time that he had been rescued from Shephelah to no ordinary nation and that Darak and his wife were no ordinary citizens of it. He could not help but wonder if his discovery had not been an accident at all. Could it be that Darak had been sent to search for him? Had the Lion and his Commanders initiated the search? Was he already expected at the Stronghold? In some strange way he suspected that he might be.

When the tall towers of Theotes came into view Amrach felt himself grow weak. Though they were still some distance from the Stronghold he became aware of an inner struggle. Part of him wanted to return, yet another part of him was magnetically drawn towards it. His heart pounded. His pulse raced.

'It's all right, my friend. I know just how you feel. All who have reached this point on the approach experience exactly what you are experiencing now. It is nothing strange. In fact it is to be expected. Be comforted and let us travel on.'

If only my wife and sons were able to see this sight, thought Amrach. She, his dearest companion, was gone: and the boys – who knew what they were enduring at this very moment? He dismissed the thought, not because he did not care but because he cared too much.

The Stronghold was as huge as it was splendid. Flowered terraces raced down from the base of its walls, along the lengths of lanes and thoroughfares, and hugged the sides of lakes and streams. The approach road to the castle entrance was lined with Beings in shining livery and glinting armour. Sentries stood upon its walls. Amrach somehow felt that, although they were the size and build of mortal men, their eyes could see for mile upon mile and that they had been given knowledge that was every bit as broad as their vision.

The towers were cascaded in light. Not the light of the sun, but effulgence that emanated from the Stronghold itself. Its rays did not dazzle nor blind him and he felt that the closer he came to the castle, their radiance brought strength and healing to his body.

'Greetings! My names is Aspasmos.'

Amrach spun around, startled. He had neither noticed or heard the figure that had drawn alongside them in his chariot. Their minds, especially Amrach's for whom this had been a first encounter, had been totally captivated by the scene that had enveloped them.

'I have been sent to greet you. The Lion awaits your coming.'

Amrach turned his head slowly towards Darak and, as their eyes met, his friend's face reflected a knowing smile.

3

The Lion and the Paraclete

Aspasmos kept his gaze fixed forward, the leather reins taut around his wrists as the two magnificent white horses hurtled with the rattling chariot nearer and nearer their destination. Entering the courtyard of the castle Aspasmos heaved back on the strong thongs and, with a cry understood only by the mighty animals themselves, brought the beasts to a standstill. As he did so a group of attendants ran forward to take charge of the shining vehicle as Aspasmos ushered Amrach and Darak into the precincts of the Stronghold itself.

All of Amrach's senses were stirred as his mind tried to take in something of the scene that lay before him. It was not just that he had never seen anything like this before – he could never even have imagined it. His ears rang with the sound of singing; music that, though he had never heard the like before did not appear to him to be either alien or strange.

What captivated his attention first was the Lion himself, seated at the far end of the huge hall on a golden throne. He seemed to be both far away and, at the same time, incredibly near. The sight of him filled Amrach with awe yet not with dread, and at that moment he remembered the words of Darak: that to meet him was both the easiest and yet the hardest thing in the world.

'Who are these around the throne?' whispered Amrach to Darak as they drew nearer.

'To the left are those who worship the Lion both day and night: and beside them are his Commanders who rush to do his bidding.'

'And the women?'

'They are the Daughters of Zohah, but silence now; the Lion is about to speak.'

'And you are Amrach?'

The Lion's voice seemed to fill the whole hall and far beyond. Aspasmos and Darak drew to one side as if for that moment their mission was completed. Now all eyes were on Amrach as he stood, a solitary figure, in the centre of the towering chamber.

'I am Amrach, your Majesty.' Amrach did not know whether to go on, or to wait until the Lion bade him proceed. The silence that followed his short statement spurred him on to continue.

'I have travelled for many miles . . .' Amrach continued his story and noticed that, as he spoke, never once did the Lion's eyes move their attention from him. The Lion seemed not so much to be looking at him, as looking through him. He felt that, although concentrating on him, the Lion was not hearing anything that he did not know. It was as if the Lion was not listening to Amrach's words at all, but listening to Amrach the man. As he concluded his story it seemed that not only his words had been understood, but that he as an individual was, in some way, also 'known'. And, experiencing that, he was totally convinced that anything that he might think or feel in the future – this too would be known to the Lion.

'And what would you have me do for you, Amrach? What is your request of me?'

'Sire, only you can drive back the Princes of Harag and their armies. No mortal has the power to withstand them.'

Amrach felt his heart beat even faster. Could it be that the Lion would not accede to his request? Was this to be a fruitless journey? Were the Princes of Harag and their bloodline really invincible – even against the Lion?

'How long have you been in Phos, Amrach?'

'I cannot be sure your Majesty. You see . . .' Amrach turned around hoping to be prompted by Darak and it was only then that he realised that Darak and Aspasmos were no longer by his side. They were part of the crowd that filled the hall but he was unable to pick them out from where he stood. He could not remember how long he had lain in Darak's house before he had regained consciousness and, as he turned his head back towards the Lion, he heard him continue.

'If you had been here for any length of time you would have been aware of the way that I and my Commanders work. Our ways are older than the hills yet fresher than tomorrow. You may never come to understand them, Amrach, as long as you live – but in learning them is the doorway to life and the entrance to eternity.'

'There was a time when nothing in the universe existed except the Stronghold of Theotes and those that lived therein. It was in those days that the great Strategy of Theotes was devised. The Great Council declared that, in generations to come, the power of Theotes would not work so much for man as through man. And so, brave Amrach . . .'

Amrach felt anything but brave.

'And so, brave Amrach, it is the will of the Lion that an army will advance against the Princes of Harag – but it is not I that shall raise the army. It is you. I charge you,

Amrach, to travel the length and breadth of my Kingdom – through its towns, its villages and its hamlets. Nowhere shall be closed to you. Go in my name and with my authority.'

The Lion motioned to one of his attendants, who stepped forward carrying a purple cushion. It was not until he was within a short distance that Amrach saw what lay upon it – a Silver Sceptre – an ornate rod that was only held by those of royal blood. And then he remembered the words of Darak, 'It is better never to take hold of the Sceptre than to take hold of it and then lay it down.'

By now the Lion's attendant was directly in front of him. Not a soul stirred in the Great Hall. For what seemed like an eternity, Amrach stood captivated by the sight of the Sceptre. Should he take it? Though it looked delicate and light, how heavy would it prove to be?

'You seem to be uncertain,' interjected the Lion. 'That is not a bad thing. You do well to consider the great responsibility before you. Tell me, of what are you afraid?'

Freeing his eyes for a moment from the Sceptre and turning again towards the Lion, Amrach confessed, 'I am afraid, Sire, that I will not be equal to the task.'

'You are not commencing your journey here, Amrach. Your journey started the moment you became a guardian of the Remnant Legend.'

'You know of that?' gasped Amrach.

'I have watched you over the years and, if you can believe it, I knew you before you were born. You have been diligent to this point yet, if you accept the Sceptre, I must warn you that many challenges lie ahead. If you will go, I will ensure that one of the Council of Theotes will travel with you. I will send the Paraclete. You may consult with him at all times. He will convey to you my mind and will never leave your side day or night.'

'Where will I find he who is called the Paraclete?'

At this, laughter rang throughout the Great Hall. It was not the laughter of mockery; it was kind in its tone. Amrach's eyes darted from face to face, searching for some small clue as to why what he had said had caused such a response.

The Lion smiled. 'The mighty Paraclete is here with us now though you cannot see him. He and I, together with the Great Invisible One, comprise the Council of Theotes.'

'If you accept the Silver Sceptre, he will be there when you wake and when you sleep. When you ride, he will ride with you.'

'Forgive me Sire, how will I know that he is there if I cannot see him? How can I be comforted if I am not aware of his presence?'

'You will discover, Amrach, that neither his power or his presence is determined by what you feel, or by your natural sight. You must learn to trust, Amrach – you must learn to trust.'

'Then, your Majesty, I will take the Silver Sceptre.'

At this the assembled crowd burst into applause and the Great Hall resounded with celebration, music and song. Amrach, took the Sceptre firmly in his hands, bowed before the Lion, and walked slowly backwards until he was within a short distance of the large door of the Hall. It was there that he was joined by Aspasmos and Darak. Aspasmos spoke first.

'I have been instructed to grant you both lodgings and food for as long as you wish to stay in the precincts of the Stronghold. You probably have many questions, and I will help you if I can. I understand, of course, that you may wish to get on your way as soon as possible – you to your family, Darak, and you, Amrach, on your mission.'

It had never occurred to Amrach that he and Darak would be parting company, and that his new friend would not be accompanying him on his journey. Looking across the room, he saw that Darak's face mirrored a similar sadness. He realised of course that Darak must return to his wife and his home now that he had fulfilled his responsibility. The introduction to the Lion had been made.

For the first time since the tragic events of the past weeks, Amrach began to feel an awful sense of loneliness edging in on him. When he had first set off across the Plains of Shephelah his thoughts had been primarily of escape. Later, fatigued and despondent, he had not been in a state to think lucidly about anything. From the point that his recovery had begun, all his attention had been on the possibility of an encounter with the Lion.

'Well,' said Aspasmos stepping in helpfully, 'what if we were to get ourselves something to eat and continue our conversation over a meal?' They nodded and followed him as he led the way.

The meal over, Amrach enquired of Aspasmos:

'You know, one thing that puzzles me is how I am going to be able to make contact with the Paraclete. Should there not have been some form of introduction? I appreciate that I cannot see him – but how will I know that he is there?'

'Oh, he will always be there – have no fear of that. But there are some things that you should be aware of. It will seem strange to you at first, but you will soon come to realise that the Paraclete will never speak about himself: only of the Lion. He will never tell you what his will is, but only of the will of the Lion. It will take a bit of getting used to, to begin with – but before too long it will appear to be the most natural thing in the world.'

'Another thing, the Silver Sceptre – how am I to carry it? It does not seem too heavy but what do you advise?'

'You will find with the Sceptre', said Aspasmos, 'that its weight will change even from day to day. There will be times when you will find it almost too heavy to bear, and times when you will forget that you are carrying it at all.'

And with that, Aspasmos explained that it was time to bid them farewell. He saluted them both, turned, and was gone

'Well,' said Amrach, 'the time has now come for us also to say goodbye. You must return to your home and I must set out on my journey. I hope that we will meet again good Darak. Were it not for your wife and yourself I would not be here today. It is far beyond me to repay the debt I owe you. Whatever will face me in the future, I want you to know that you will always be in my thoughts, and I trust that I will be in yours.'

As they rose from the table Darak put his hand on his friend's shoulder. 'I am sure that we will meet again sometime. When, or how, I do not know. Be strong, Amrach. Never doubt the presence of the Paraclete or the strength of the Lion. When the Sceptre seems heavier hold it firmer; when the strong winds that sometimes sweep across the land of Phos try to drive you from your course, hold the more steadfastly to your path.'

Amrach and Darak left together and re-traced their steps along the road to the outer perimeter of the Stronghold. Coming to a crossroads, they embraced and went their separate ways.

Amrach thought it strange that Darak, knowing he was a total stranger to the land of Phos, had offered him neither map nor directions. He had not so much as even suggested a route that he might take. He concluded however that it could not have been thoughtlessness on

Darak's part, but that there must be some hidden reason that he was not yet aware of. Why else would he leave him without guidance, money, or a mount in a place where there was neither friend or stranger in sight?

'I wonder where I will encounter the Paraclete?' thought Amrach as he strode purposefully along a path that edged its way beside a forest. He struck on the thought that it might be an idea to call out for the Paraclete in order to summon him. So, putting his hands either side of his mouth, arching his back and throwing back his head, he shouted the name of the Paraclete into the early evening air.

'You have no need to bellow my name. Even a whisper will suffice.'

Amrach spun round on his heels so fast that he almost lost his balance.

'Do not try to look for me. You will never see me with your natural eye – but I am with you just the same. Draw aside for a moment from the road and we will talk together. Yes, I am the Paraclete, the one the Lion told you would be accompanying you wherever you go. When you need direction, I will be your guide and when you encounter error I will show you the truth. You have a long journey ahead of you and I have already charted your course.'

'Tell me,' said Amrach excitedly, 'what are your plans for me? Tell me something of what lies ahead and name the places to which my quest will take me.'

'It is not so much a case of "places" but of "place". You will not be told too far in advance what your direction is to be. You will be led step by step, and only as you advance in obedience to the will of the Lion will you be able to see further along the road you are to take.'

'And all I have to do is to whisper your name?' enquired Amrach.

'No, not my name; in future I will respond to you whenever you call upon the name of the Lion.'

'But surely he is in the Stronghold?' retorted Amrach.

'The Lion is everywhere,' rebuked the Paraclete gently. 'You see, I have been sent to you with his authority and with his total power. When you use my power in the Lion's name you will be as strong as the Lion himself. Though you may enquire of me at any time, it would be best if we spoke together early each day before you set off on your mission. Before too long it will be dusk and the night will be drawing in. If you enter the forest ahead while it is still light and take the centre path, you will eventually come to a cottage. I have requested a man called Berekah to give you shelter for the night and provisions for tomorrow.'

Much encouraged by his conversation with the Paraclete, Amrach set off along the road in the direction of the forest. Almost before he left the road to look for the middle path he noticed that the daylight was drawing in and that the way ahead was noticeably darker. He negotiated the middle path without too much difficulty and was glad that he had spoken to the Paraclete and had received instruction from him before night had fully fallen.

It was not too long before yellow light, streaming across the path before him, indicated the precise position of the cottage. The door was opened by an old man carrying a short candle, who smiled broadly at his visitor.

'Berekah?' enquired Amrach.

'Yes indeed – and you, good traveller, must be Amrach. The Paraclete told me that you would be coming. Step inside and take a seat by my fire while I continue to light the lamps around the house.'

As Amrach entered, his eyes were drawn towards a log fire that crackled and glowed amidst a red-bricked hearth. On the stone wall above the hearth were fastened pieces of hunting equipment fashioned in wood and iron. There were two seats, one on either side of the fire, and Amrach wondered which one it would be polite to choose. Perhaps one of them was special to his host.

Although Berekah was in another room continuing to light his lamps, as if aware of Amrach's dilemma he called out, 'Sit anywhere you choose and I will join you in just a moment.'

Amrach sank deep into the welcoming comfort of the chair to the right of the hearth, and was soon joined around the log fire by the owner of the cottage.

'Welcome to my home, Amrach.'

'Thank you – the people of Phos must be the most hospitable in the universe. I do not know if I have known such kindness anywhere that I have travelled. The problem is that I am not in any position to repay you. The whole thing is an embarrassment to me, really it is.'

'Listen, Amrach, you will repay us all well enough if your mission is successful and you are able to raise an army that will stand against the Princes of Harag.'

'You know about my mission then?' said Amrach with surprise.

'Oh, yes – when the Paraclete requested me to give you shelter for the night he told me of it. Creatures and men of all kinds pass through the forest at night, and the Paraclete doubtless felt it would be a comfort to me to know not only the name, but also the assignment of the one who would come under my roof.'

'I understand,' said Amrach, knowingly. 'Do you give hospitality often, and to many travellers?'

'I open my home to as many as the Paraclete brings to my door.' Berekah turned his head towards the fire and looked, as if searching for something, into its glowing

embers. 'My heart has been warmed many a time as I
have met those who have passed this way: warriors,
sages, prophets, nobles, the rich and the poor. There is
many a story that I could tell and many a memory to
keep me company in the time between.'

The two of them talked well into the night – the old
man recalling the stories of valiant men and women and
fallen heroes and telling tales of good times and of bad.
Amrach then related the account of his adventures thus
far. He knew, as he spoke, that Berekah was adding this
as the latest jewel in his treasure chest of recollections.
He concluded with the words: 'And that is how I came
to the home of Darak.'

At this, the face of the old man lit up once again with
the smile that had first greeted Amrach at the door.

'Darak,' said Berekah with a sigh, savouring the name
as if tasting a morsel of the best food.

'You know of him too, then?' said Amrach, surprised.

'I most certainly do. You would be hard pressed to find
a worthy man around here that doesn't. Surely you are
aware, if you have spent time with him, that he is one of
the Lion's most loyal and courageous Commanders!'

'Darak? That can't be. Darak looks so ordinary and
conducts himself with such humility. He has no robes of
officialdom. You must surely be thinking of someone
else with the same name.'

'Oh no, there is no mistake. You can be sure that we
are talking about the same person. It is not unusual for
the Lion's Commanders to divest themselves of the
tokens of their importance and live, in every respect, as
ordinary men.'

'But why then, did Darak not tell me of this while I
was with him?'

'Why should he? What difference would that have
made to you? Would you have been better rescued if he

had gone, at the request of the Lion, to deliver you from the Plains of Shephelah dressed in an ornate uniform? Would you have been more comfortable in his home if he had introduced himself to you by some grand title? I think not,' said Berekah.

'I suppose not,' conceded Amrach, somewhat rebuked. 'I have been in Phos such a short time and I confess I find it a stranger place by the day.'

'And you will find it stranger yet,' said the old man. 'But now for some supper and then we will retire for the night so you will be rested, refreshed and able to face the journey that lies ahead.'

The two of them ate a fine meal, almost too good to sleep on. They talked a little more and then, when both felt fully tired, Berekah showed Amrach to his room.

4

The Blacksmith's Forge

Amrach woke early the next morning with the memory of the Paraclete's advice that they speak with one another early. Knowing that it is was through this encounter that he discovered the mind of the Council of Theotes, he called for the Lion.

'The will of the Lion today,' began the Paraclete, 'is that you head for the town of Chaneph which lies some half day's journey to the north. Feel free to tell them of your vision and relate to them openly how vital it is that an army be formed to face the threat posed by the Princes of Harag.'

'Will I travel the distance by foot, and what of the supplies that I will need for the way ahead?' asked Amrach.

'You have nothing to worry about. Provisions will be supplied as and when you require them; they will never come too early and never too late. I have spoken to Berekah about your needs for today. Everything has been taken care of.'

Washed and dressed, Amrach drew his few belongings together and headed in the direction of the smell of cooking and the sizzling sound that proved to be coming from the kitchen.

'I trust you slept well?' enquired Berekah.

'Yes indeed, though I woke early.'

'And have you spoken with the Paraclete?' asked the old man.

'I have, and he tells me that once more I am to be in your debt.'

'Debt does not enter into it,' said Berekah as he emptied the hot contents of a pan onto a plate that had been set aside for Amrach.

'No one has ever out-given the Council of Theotes,' he continued. 'A person always ends up the richer for the giving.'

Breakfast over, Amrach expressed his thanks to the old man. As he was about to leave, Berekah pressed into his hands a leather pouch with the words, 'There are enough gold pieces in there to keep you going for a while and, by the way, a surprise for you . . .'

It was then that Amrach saw it. Before him was a dapple grey horse with a long flowing mane. Amrach took to it immediately.

'As you see, it is saddled and ready for the journey. I have given it no name. I have left that for you to do. You will find it steady over rough terrain yet swift and fleet of foot in battle. Farewell Amrach. May the power of the Paraclete ride with you as you go.'

Amrach mounted the horse, waved goodbye to Berekah and, gripping the reins in both hands, headed north along the middle road and through the forest.

'And what shall you be called then, my new friend?' said Amrach as he ventured his mount from trot to canter. 'I think I shall name you Morning Breeze – yes, that is what you shall be called.' As if emphasising a good decision the two of them, to the percussion of racing hooves, moved into a gallop until the edge of the forest was reached.

As they came to open meadow Amrach gazed at the surrounding landscape from the higher than usual vantage point of his saddle. Mile after mile of verdant pasture spread out before them. Acres of green met his eyes, patch-worked only by thin lines of grey stone walls and silvery threads of clear water identifying the courses of rivulets and streams. His shoulders rose as he filled every corner of his lungs with morning air. Hardly a cloud could be seen against the bright blue sky, though in places the occasional puff of white scudded compli antly in the prevailing wind.

The Sceptre, wrapped in cloth and slung by a leather thong across his back, had never felt lighter. He was hardly aware of its weight and, at moments like this, he was near to forgetting that he was carrying it at all. But carrying it he was, and this fact prodded him into resuming his journey northwards.

Amrach travelled for some time without seeing another living soul. The only sounds that had met his ears since leaving Berekah's cottage were the trotting hooves of his horse, the singing of the birds as they darted and fluttered in the trees around him and the sporadic clicking of invisible crickets in the hedgerows by the side of the lane.

Now however, as he crossed a bridge that spanned a small stream, he heard the sound of hammer upon metal. It came from a small building with whitewashed walls which he later discovered was the home of a Blacksmith. Amrach felt overdue for a break and so, dismounting his horse and tying its reins to a post, he made his way in the direction of the noise that greatly increased in volume as he approached it.

'Anybody in?' asked Amrach – a silly question, he thought, as soon as the enquiry left his lips.

There were two men in the working area which he entered. The first was the Blacksmith himself. He was a tall and thick set man with muscular arms. Amrach thought that he could have guessed his occupation in whatever environment he would have met him. The second was different in almost every way – a small, dumpy, overweight person whose most distinguishing feature was his squint eyes. Though in many ways his features were grotesque, he did not give Amrach any sense of foreboding. There was something mischievous about him – almost comical.

'I see you have a horse out there. Is it fresh shoes that you are looking for?'

The Blacksmith asked his question, his hammer poised aloft as if frozen in space in such a way that it could only be permitted its downward path at a response from the stranger.

'No, not at all, the horse is fine thank you,' Amrach stammered. He could hardly say that he had stopped off by way of a rest from travelling but, as he rummaged for a suitable excuse for imposing himself upon them, the man with squint eyes came to his rescue.

'Travelled far, chummy?'

Amrach was unsure as to whether he liked being addressed as 'chummy'. But he was relieved to be able to deflect for a moment the attention of the Blacksmith, whose towering arm had long since come down on the red hot metal that lay astride the anvil, and he was happy to respond.

'I have been travelling for most of the morning but, as you can probably tell from my accent, I do not originate from these parts.'

'Well, where do you "originate" from, chummy?' volleyed back the squint-eyed man.

'I have come a long way, from the west: from the pasture lands.'

'That means that you must have crossed the Plains of Shephelah to get here,' enjoined the Blacksmith.

'Yes indeed,' said Amrach feeling that the exchanges were veering all too quickly from conversation to interrogation for his liking.

The man with squint eyes, who to this point had been poised precariously on a stool and had been nursing in his hands a chipped mug of questionable content, drew himself up to his full size – not greatly different, it appeared to Amrach, from his previous posture. It was clear that he wanted to get a better view of the stranger who had interrupted their morning conversation.

'The truth is,' offered Amrach, 'that I am on the way to Chaneph.'

'You'll be going for the annual feast then, that starts tomorrow,' suggested the Blacksmith.

'Feast? I know nothing about that. Is it to mark a special event of some kind?'

The squint-eyed man pushed the chipped mug towards Amrach with the words,

'If you will join me in a little Honeydew, I will be more than happy to tell you about it. By the way, my name is Tumbleweed.'

Amrach was uncertain of many things that lay before him in the weeks and months to come. But there was one thing of which he was totally sure and that was, of all the things that he desired for himself, joining Tumbleweed in a little Honeydew was not among them. He raised his hand in a gesture that made his point and Tumbleweed drew the mug back across the table toward him.

'There are not too many that would turn down my good old Honeydew, chummy,' uttered Tumbleweed somewhat hurt. 'I'll have you know that it has made me the man I am today.'

Amrach was sure that he was right.

It was evident that the Blacksmith had finished the project before him. He drew up an old chair and, pointing

Amrach to a similar one, indicated that he might join them both for a while.

'Oh, the Feast of Chaneph takes me back,' reminisced the Blacksmith, attempting to make himself more comfortable on the rickety chair.

'We used to go every year, the family and I. But nowadays I don't bother too much – not like I used to, anyway.'

Amrach searched the man's face to work out the meaning behind his last statement, and what he saw was a mixture of sadness and disappointment mingled perhaps with just a little guilt.

'The fact is that it is very much a religious festival, as is widely known, and I feel that that sort of thing is for far worthier fellows than me. I was involved in the goings on in Chaneph in years gone by but not so much now. I have to say that I have been occupied with other things. You might even call them shady dealings.'

The Blacksmith looked over to Tumbleweed thinking that perhaps he might say something in his defence – suggesting that perhaps the adjective 'shady' might be too harsh a word to use. Instead, Tumbleweed, cocking his head to one side as if to intone the perfect nuance of the word enjoined, 'Shady? Yes, I think that that's about the right word for them, "shady".'

'Then this is a religious festival?' asked Amrach, his eyes darting between the two of them in order to draw out a reply from either one.

'Yes chummy, it marks of one of the Lion's greatest victories – one that took place many years ago. Each year a celebration is held and singers, poets, actors and dancers re-enact the wonderful event, accompanied by the masterly musicians of Chaneph. They are renowned for their musicians, chummy, renowned.'

'Well in that case I could not have come here at a better time,' said Amrach. 'I . . .' He paused to heighten the importance of what was to come next, 'I have come here to raise an army on behalf of the Lion himself and, if given the chance, will proclaim to the town the reason for my mission. And what better time of year to do it than the Feast, while the exploits of the Lion are in everyone's mind.'

The Blacksmith and Tumbleweed exchanged the briefest of glances. Their eye-contact was so short that Amrach thought that he may have imagined it. It was as if they shared some common knowledge denied to him and which they were reticent to pass on.

Narrowing his squint eyes even more, Tumbleweed said, 'I for one wish you well, but do not let your hopes rise too high.'

Amrach thought it unwise to press the matter further. Instead, he enquired as to whether the Blacksmith and his friend would be joining the celebrations this year.

'I can't be sure, myself,' said the Blacksmith. 'As I explained earlier, I feel a bit of a hypocrite, especially with all those religious folk. Tumbleweed will be going though; the food is free.'

'It occurs to me,' said Tumbleweed benignly, 'that as you are not familiar with the land of Phos, it may be in your best interest if I were to travel along with you. I had intended to go to the Feast tomorrow, but as the two of us have now met up – doubtless providence has ordained it – I am sure that that would be to your liking, would it not?'

Amrach felt that providence stood in the dock falsely accused of this charge, but there was little reason that he could think of for not allowing him to join him on the road.

'That's settled then, chummy,' enthused Tumbleweed. 'You shall have the benefit of my company all the way to Chaneph and I shall have the honour of conducting you to a most admirable hostelry where we can spend the night.'

Amrach hardly liked to imagine the kind of inn with which Tumbleweed would be familiar but was sure that, wherever it was, it would be a major dispenser of Honeydew.

They mounted their horses and made for the north. Tumbleweed proved to be far better company than Amrach had imagined. So good in fact, that they arrived in the vicinity of Chaneph much sooner than either of them had expected – not because the distance was shorter but because of the lively conversation on the way.

'We'll find a good selection of inns to the east of the town,' said Tumbleweed, 'so if you will be good enough to follow me, I will lead the way.'

What a procession! A short man astride an undersized and over-nourished horse of indeterminate parentage was followed by Amrach – riding the thoroughbred that, since the beginning of the day, had rejoiced in the name of Morning Breeze.

A lad approached them as they entered the courtyard of the inn and proceeded to offer to feed and water their horses for the night, assuring them that their animals would be well bedded in a clean stable with fresh straw. And so, handing the horses over, Amrach and Tumbleweed booked themselves two rooms.

When the innkeeper came to enquire how long the visitors expected to stay it was readily apparent that he recognised the shorter of the two immediately. It was furthermore of no surprise to either of them that Tumbleweed, having rummaged for his purse, should utter an oath to the effect that he must have left the said pouch back at the Blacksmith's forge. He then sought to elicit from Amrach an answer to his request to the tune of a golden piece – just until he was at liberty to repay him, of course.

Though he did not believe his story for a moment, Amrach was happy to oblige. After all, everything in his possession had been made available to him through the kindness of Berekah after the prompting of the Paraclete.

Taking the money with an air of feigned embarrassment, Tumbleweed excused himself on the grounds that he must counsel some poor souls who lodged at the inn and who would, if hearing he was here, doubtless require his succour and support.

Amrach and the innkeeper exchanged a smile. Both of them had seen from the corner of their eyes, a group of Tumbleweed's cronies waving him towards the opposite end of the Tavern.

5

The Feast of Chaneph

Amrach slept only fitfully. The noise of the inn below his bedroom kept him awake during the first part of the night and, once that was over, his mind raced with the challenge that rose before him – the first opportunity that he had had to inspire the population of a town to join him in his quest.

He left the inn while the dawn was still breaking, to roam the roads and get his bearings while the town was still empty. The coloured bunting that lined the streets in preparation for the day's celebrations hung cold and damp and swayed only gently in the early breeze. Amrach knew that just a few hours later it would glitter gloriously when the sun rose to highlight its brightness to its best advantage.

It appeared that some others had also taken the opportunity to take an early stroll and a few nodded to Amrach as they passed. It then occurred to him that he had not yet spoken with the Paraclete, and instinctively he looked back in the direction of the inn as if he had left him there.

'It is all right, Amrach,' said the Paraclete. 'I am not just to be found in any one place. The first time we spoke was along a country road and the next time it was in the cottage of Berekah. Now we are together in the centre of the town of Chaneph.'

'I really am sorry,' apologised Amrach, 'I had every intention of seeking the mind of the Lion but, I did not sleep very well and . . .'

'Enough of that – I understand. You must remember that I am not only with you during the times we talk together. I am with you at all times. I was with you in the Blacksmith's Forge just as much as I am present with you now.'

'Today,' the Paraclete went on, 'will be an important encounter for you. It will be the first real test of your strength. The festivities here take place from the middle of the afternoon. Almost every family in Chaneph will be present – men and women, young and old. They will then gather for the Feast in the early evening after which the main event of the day will take place. This will last well into the night. Story tellers and actors will relate the great deeds of the Lion. Poets and dancers will extol his praise and the wonders of the Great Invisible One. Then it will be time for you to speak.'

'Me?' gasped Amrach.

'Well yes, of course; surely that is why you have come: to speak of the raising of an army?'

'Yes – but I had not realised that I was to address the whole of the town at once. I had hoped that I might commence with small groups and then well perhaps . . . work up to towns eventually.'

'I have already instructed a leading Sage in Chaneph to introduce you at the climax of the Festival. He has not been told of the content of your message – only that it is my wish that the people give you audience.'

Exactly as the Paraclete had described, the people began to gather from shortly after noon, though not in the centre of the town as Amrach had thought. On the outskirts of Chaneph was a large natural amphitheatre, a huge grassy hollow. It was on the side of its green slopes that the people came to sit and wait for the festivities to commence.

A long, rocky plateau on the opposite side from where Amrach now stood was where he imagined those taking part would be assembled and, as time went by, he was proved right. In the middle of the plateau an imposing wooden dais had been erected.

The Blacksmith, he remembered, had told him that the town was particularly famous for its skilled musicians. Within a short space of time, hundreds of them filled the plateau until not a space could be seen.

He watched the performers as they passed him to take their places. Their costumes were consistently similar in white and gold. Amrach noticed two types of lyre: the Barbiton and the larger Phorminx. Some carried with them the Krotola, or 'clappers' as the children called them, and still others the double pipes which were named the Aulos. Trumpets, harps, handbells, tambourines and tabors made up the rest of the instruments. Poets were dressed in long green robes with the dancers in yellow and blue.

There was in evidence a sense of excitement and anticipation among the crowds who came to celebrate the most important day of the year. The buzz and chatter of conversation between friends, mingling with the noise of musicians tuning their instruments, made for a strange sound.

Amrach knew that something was about to happen when he noticed the noise of preparation fading noticeably away. His eyes followed the turning heads of the multitude now assembled as they fixed their attention on the central dais. For it was to this focal point that the

Sage of Chaneph approached. Total silence was observed as he began to speak, and Amrach was surprised at how well his voice carried. He was not a little nervous as he realised that, before the day would come to a close, this great crowd would become his audience.

The Sage spoke slowly and clearly.

'I welcome you all to the great Feast of Chaneph. This is the most sacred day in our calendar and all will find a welcome here. There will be singing, there will be dancing; there will be feasting But in all of this we must not lose sight of the real reason of our gathering. We are here in celebration of the Lion!'

This detonated a tumultuous response from the crowd. They cheered and danced, they jumped and shouted. The Sage raised his hand and the music commenced. As the multitude recognised the opening bars they cheered even louder and then, en masse, began to sing:

> Hail to the Lion, Mighty King
> And Victor over all his foes!
> From sea to sea his people come
> To give him praise and to adore.
> What tongue can tell or lips recite
> The Greatness of his name?
> From coast to coast the nations tell
> His splendour and his fame!

Only in the Great Hall of the Lion himself had Amrach heard such sounds. The song was sung over and over again. Louder and louder they praised and extolled the glory of the Lion.

'So what do you think of this, Amrach?'

Amrach swung around to the right and to the left. Though there were people around him, it was not from their direction that the voice came.

'It is I, the Paraclete,' the voice continued. 'What do you think of this?'

'Amazing, truly amazing,' replied Amrach. 'I was only just thinking that never, since the Lion's Great Hall, have I heard such rapturous worship.'

'Guard your heart, Amrach, for all is not as it seems.'

'But . . .' Even as Amrach began, he sensed that the Paraclete had said all that he was going to say and that it would be fruitless to enquire further into those incongruous words.

The period before the Feast was designated to the consecration of the Festival. That concluded, the crowds made their way back to the centre of the town. The middle of every main thoroughfare was lined with tables which ached and groaned under the weight of food upon them. There were meats of every kind. Hogs' heads garnished with apples and trimmings acted as decorations as well as food. Whole sides of beef and mutton turned on spits at the side of the roads and, once cooked, slices and joints of the choicest parts were carried to the table. Breads, cheeses, fruit and vegetables were all in abundance.

Any other day Amrach would have joined in with all his might: but the thought of addressing the crowd later on that evening, stole away any appetite that he had.

The feasting lasted for several hours and then, to the sound of trumpets, the people were summoned back to the great green hollow.

As Amrach made his way once again to the amphitheatre he noticed how fast the night was drawing in. Reaching his destination, he saw that tall and flaming torches had been lit at equal distances in the surrounding fields. The whole area, and especially along the plateau, was bathed in light.

After some initial singing, the Sage introduced the poets who were applauded as they climbed the dais. As the noise of their welcome diminished one of their number began:

> Long ago in ages past
> Across the mighty oceans vast
> Came men with minds to fight.
> They fell on every town and city
> Devoid of mercy and of pity
> With axes sharp and voices gritty
> Their kiss a serpent's bite.
>
> Fear and dread filled every heart
> Tearing homes and towns apart
> They ravaged all our land.
> They came with every rolling wave
> And though our citizens were brave
> They forced us to become their slaves
> An evil, violent band.
>
> Though great in number were the dead
> Survivors to the Lion fled
> Petitions to him came.
> The Council of Theotes, three
> With edict and proclaimed decree
> Sent armies over land and sea
> The ruthless hoard to tame.

Amrach listened as the poet continued and he was followed by others who recounted, in verses of their own, the great exploits of the Lion and the Council of Theotes. A good deal more singing followed before the Sage addressed the assembled gathering.

'Friends, we will shortly be coming to the end of our celebrations, and yet the grand finale of our festival has not yet been reached. I have been informed by the Paraclete himself . . .'

At the mention of the Paraclete an almost tangible silence swept across the people and Amrach, as swiftly and unobtrusively as he could, made his way towards the dais.

'I have been informed by the Paraclete', the Sage continued, 'that there is one among us who has travelled far to be with us this day in order to address the citizens of Chaneph.'

By now Amrach had reached the base of the dais. It looked far higher now that he was close to it, and looked out across the sea of faces. The night was dark and, though the moon gave some light, it was the long torches that provided him with a sense of distance and of depth. Yellow flickering light picked out best those who sat nearest to their golden glow.

The Sage continued, 'I ask that you will all give ear to our visitor. His name is Amrach and he comes from the land far to the west.'

He then motioned to Amrach, indicating that he should climb the dais.

The people gave the unknown speaker a warm reception and, amid the applause Amrach was aware of a shuffling as people changed their position in readiness for the anticipated speech.

'People of Chaneph, I greet you,' Amrach began. 'This has been a full day for you all and I shall not keep you any longer than necessary, though what I have to say is a great and heavy matter. The weight of what I must bring before you lies not in the importance of the speaker for, as you can see, I am but an ordinary man. Its worth and significance is found within the gravity of the message that I have been commissioned to convey.

'It was not long ago that I enjoyed the community and fellowship of Feast Days such as this in my own country. That was until our land was attacked by raiding bands that brought death and misery in their wake. Not long ago, as a result of their actions, my wife was killed and my sons enslaved. Yet it is not on my own behalf that I stand before you. I come to bring you warning. The destruction that the Princes of Harag have inflicted upon our population will not end there. It is no secret that their next objective is to cross the Plains and they will not be satisfied until every city, town and village has been brought under their despotic rule.

'You may respond that nations have fought with nations over the centuries and that battles have been lost and won before. But I am speaking here of a race different from anything that you have previously known. The Princes of Harag are as vile as they are violent. Only those who have suffered under their oppressive heel know what it is to endure their administration.

'I call, on this great day when you have been remembering the past exploits of the Lion, for many hundreds of you to join with me: to raise an army, to set ourselves against their demonic warriors, to hold out for truth and righteousness, to—'

To his utter amazement, Amrach was interrupted at this point by calls from among the crowd for him to sit down and be silent. Thinking them to be unrepresentative of the majority, he watched to see if stewards would silence the hecklers so that he might continue. But the only movement that he witnessed was those on the edge of the crowd who picked up their belongings and left.

Amrach turned round and looked for support from the Sage, who, being aware of the disturbance, had climbed the dais and was now standing a little to his left. As the heckling gathered momentum the Sage whispered in his ear:

'Er… this has become somewhat difficult. It may be best if you step down just now and I will take over and perhaps draw the proceedings to a close.'

'Step down I will not,' said Amrach defiantly. 'You well know that the Paraclete has decreed that I be given the opportunity to speak to the people of Chaneph about the impending invasion.'

'I am well aware of what the Paraclete has said,' retorted the Sage indignantly, 'but that is not the point. We are celebrating victories here today' – and he said the next three words slowly and with deliberation – 'of times past.'

'These are designed to be joyous occasions, not opportunities for worrying our poor citizens. They have had little enough to cheer them throughout the year and will not respond well to this day of celebration ending on what only can be described as a negative and sour note.'

Amrach could not believe the evidence of his ears.

'Look,' he implored, 'give me just a few moments more. Allow me to state my case before these people. They, like the rest of the land of Phos, lie in danger. Even now as we speak the bloodline of Harag may be marshalling their forces at our borders.'

'Well, if you must,' acquiesced the Sage, 'but please be as brief as you can.'

Amrach raised his hands to signal to the people that he wanted to continue.

'People of Chaneph listen to me—'

There was chaos in the crowd, yet Amrach still tried to make his voice heard above the tumult.

'I have come to your town today as a stranger, as a visitor. I have listened to your singing in praise of the Lion and have paid attention to your poets as they have shared, with eloquence, your gratitude to him. It is because of all that I have heard this day that I am amazed that you will not give me your full attention. I implore you to take heed to the danger that you are in. Think not only of days gone by but think of your future and the future of your children. Consider the threat of cruel armies – even now you lie within their embrace.'

'I'd rather succumb to the embrace of a warm bed at this time of night!' came one retort that was accompanied by derisive laughter from every corner of the crowd.

Amrach's voice grew fainter and his features, picked out by flames from the surrounding torches, became a canvas coloured by disappointment and disbelief.

'All I will say to you then is this: while you make merriment of my words, you make a greater mockery of yourselves. Your musicians have played skilfully and your poets spoken eloquently, but in reality all is emptiness and dross. If there are any worthy among you let them stay to speak to me afterward . . .' Amrach looked round urgently for some rallying point before he continued, 'by that large oak tree over there.'

By now the uproar had degenerated into almost total anarchy, and at this point it was the Sage who sought to take control.

'I am sorry about this, people of Chaneph; I had no way of knowing what this fellow Amrach was about to say. I was informed only that he would speak, and not of the content of his message. All I can ask of you, as you travel to your homes, is that you try to remember the best and most inspiring parts of the day and do all in your power to leave this last sad episode behind you.'

If Amrach had been astonished at what had happened to this point, followed by the feeble phrases that their principal religious leader had added, what was to happen next was to leave him totally dumfounded. Could he really believe what he now heard from the lips of the Sage?

'And as we go on our way let us sing again the song with which we first began the Feast day:

> Hail to the Lion, Mighty King
> And Victor over all his foes!
> From sea to sea his people come
> To give him praise and to adore.
> What tongue can tell or lips recite
> The Greatness of his name?
> From coast to coast the nations tell
> His splendour and his fame!

They sang with all the lustre of their first performance. Amrach stood silent. He heard them sing and watched them leave. He remained there as the musicians laughed and joked with one another and, having gathered their instruments together, in a while they too were gone.

Amrach remained there where he stood; his open eyes only now yielding to warm tears that ran in rivers down his face. He had wept few times in his adult years. The last time was as he bent over the battered body of his dead wife. On that occasion his grief had been for one wasted by death. Tonight he wept for thousands who had been wasted in life. How long he stood there he did not know, but his solitude was eventually broken by a voice which said:

'How long are we supposed to wait for you under this old tree, chummy?'

Tumbleweed led him to a small group that had gathered obediently around the oak. There were no more than a dozen of them. The Blacksmith was one of them and it was he that spoke first.

'I know that I am not up to much.'

'And me neither,' chorused Tumbleweed in agreement.

'But if you think that the Lion could use even people
such as us . . .'

Amrach moved into the centre of the tiny circle, his
arms outstretched as if to take them all into his embrace.

'If?' said Amrach, a gentle smile rising across his face.
'There is no "if" about it. You will each become mighty
warriors. The Lion will be proud of you.'

6

The Valley of Chanuts

Amrach could not bring himself to stay one more night in Chaneph. He told his twelve volunteers that he would return for them once his mission to raise an army from the rest of the land of Phos was completed and, bidding them farewell, stepped out into the night to reclaim his horse from the stable boy and continue on his journey.

'What direction would the Lion have me travel now?' enquired Amrach.

'You are directed to the next village, the village of Madon,' responded the Paraclete.

'A village?' questioned Amrach. 'After the experience I have had this day I would surely be better sent to a city, and to a large city at that. If I can only muster a dozen from a town, what chance will I have in a village?'

'Be careful how you speak,' counselled the Paraclete. 'It is not for you to query the will of the Lion, only to obey him. When your will crosses his will, your will must die. If you have learned anything from these past hours you must surely realise that it is better to have twelve that are fully surrendered to the Lion's will than to have a thousand that will only pay him lip service.'

'I am sorry,' answered Amrach. 'It is just that it is only now that I am beginning to feel the full weight of this Silver Sceptre. I wish only to be obedient, truly I do, to any command that will keep the forces of Harag at bay.'

'How far is it to Madon from here?'

'If your journey goes well you should make it in a day or so. You will need to cross through the Chanuts valley, and not everyone negotiates it quickly or without hindrance.'

'I hope', said Amrach, 'that I will not face the kind of rejection I have encountered today everywhere I go.'

'It is not really you that has been rejected, it is your message. And, as what you are carrying has the seal of the Lion upon it, it is he that bears the ultimate rejection. That, however, is not an experience that he is unfamiliar with and, if you will truly be his servant, you must be willing to identify yourself with him in it. You would seek to share his glory in battle would you not?'

'Yes indeed,' said Amrach.

'Well in that case, you must also be ready to share his rejection. If a messenger tears up a message before it is delivered then he is responsible to his master. If on the other hand he delivers the message and the one to whom he delivers the message destroys it – it is the recipient that bears the burden of responsibility.'

Amrach considered it strange that, even when the Paraclete rebuked him, he still felt comforted by his words. There was a great security, he thought, in knowing that there was someone who would always tell him the truth about himself, even though the revelation may hurt him for a while. The Paraclete bade him get some rest as it was now well into the early hours of the morning. He slept under the stars and, when dawn broke, continued on his way.

The sky became increasingly overcast as the day progressed and, by the time he arrived at the entrance of the

Chanuts valley, drizzle was giving way to much heavier rain. Amrach pulled up the collar of his coat in order to afford himself a little more protection but, when a westerly wind arose to give a greater cutting edge to the downpour, he found himself searching for far more substantial shelter.

In the distance he could hear the sound of an approaching horse, but due to the surrounding mist it was not until the rider was almost upon him that he was able to determine his features.

'If I were you I would get out of this as soon as you can,' suggested the stranger as he shouted above the howling wind. 'I am familiar with this area and, believe me, this can only get worse.'

'Thank you,' Amrach called back, even though the man was just a matter of feet away from him. 'Would you be so kind as to tell me where I might find some temporary refuge?'

The man's horse shifted uneasily forward and backward, obviously eager to be on its way also.

'A little way ahead you will come to a place where the entrance to the valley divides in two. To the right you will find a rough road, and to the left there is a passage that will lead you through gentler countryside. Both will bring you to the far side of the valley. My advice would be to take the road to the left, especially on a day like this.'

Amrach thanked him once again and the man rode off at speed. In a short distance Amrach came to the place where the road forked. It never once occurred to him to ask the advice of the Paraclete on the matter. It would have never entered his mind to deliberate on something as trivial as this. Had he done so, he would have concluded that it would have been obvious to anyone that the easiest route must surely be the best option.

The weather showed no sign of improving and, if anything, was getting worse. However, Amrach was encouraged by the sight of a building that lay ahead. In was clearly an inn of some kind and, having secured his horse, he ran from the pursuing storm into its entrance.

Sweeping the worst of the water from his cloak, and stamping his feet once or twice to dislodge any attending mud from his boots, he was greeted as he advanced into the room by cheery faces and by an even cheerier fire.

'Phew – what a day, what a terrible day!' said Amrach by way of introduction. 'Do you have anything hot to eat and drink? I'd give a king's ransom for it if you have.'

'We'll not be requiring a King's ransom from you, I'm sure,' responded a man who by his white – or once white – apron, Amrach assumed to have some authority in the establishment.

Had Amrach not been so intent in securing one of the vacant seats beside the fire, he would probably have noticed the furtive wink that the apron-clad man gave to a group of rough fellows already occupying one of the tables towards the corner. Though he had missed the wink, he had noticed them and had concluded that it was likely that they were used to investing not a little of their substance in this and similar hostelries in the area. Amrach chose a leather-covered chair that, though it had clearly seen better days, he felt would be more than sufficient to rest his weary limbs for a while.

One of the group left his seat and walked towards the landlord. This unspectacular event caused Amrach no concern as he assumed that his intention was to place his order for food. He would have hardly noticed him at all were it not for a large gold ring that he was wearing that glinted briefly in the candlelight as he passed. The ring was to be more significant than Amrach could have imagined for, once at the counter, the man prised open a small hinged lid in it and, unseen by Amrach, poured some powdery contents into the drink that had been prepared for him.

Amrach tucked heartily into the stew he had ordered. He had not eaten for some time due to the events of the previous day. The fare seemed to surpass anything that he had seen on the groaning tables of Chaneph. This was not due to its superior quality but because today he was hungrier than he had been for a long time.

Part way through his meal he caught the landlord's eye and nodded appreciatively to him. The man reciprocated the smile with a measure of unease, and nervously adjusted the string of his stained apron as he did so. Under normal circumstances that may have signalled some concern to him, but he was a cold man getting warmer and a hungry man becoming more satisfied and such thoughts were swept from his mind before they had a chance to take root.

The stew consumed, Amrach took the mug in his hand and then to his lips, with the air of a writer putting a full stop at the end of a well-constructed sentence. And that was all he remembered.

When he awoke from his slouched position across the table there was no sign of the mug, his empty plate, or the fire in the grate. Apart from the man in the off-white apron, the room was empty.

'How long have I been here?' enquired Amrach, dazed, his head spinning.

'A couple of hours I'd say,' returned the landlord. 'And, if I might make so bold as to say so sir, it might well be time that you were on your way. If it is a place to sleep that you are looking for I have good rooms to let at a very moderate charge. If it is not your intention to avail yourself of our hospitality may I suggest then that you take your leave?'

'I am sorry for any inconvenience that I may have caused you. If you will just let me know how much I am in your debt, I will be glad to pay and go.'

He reached into the leather pouch that Berekah had given him and groped in vain for coins.

'My gold pieces!' exclaimed Amrach.

'Gold pieces?' echoed the landlord. 'You are not surely going to say that you have consumed my fine food and drink, and are without the money to pay, sir? Do you wish to make mockery of my genial hospitality, to treat contemptuously my kind reception of you?'

'Not at all, not at all,' implored Amrach. 'It is quite evident that I have been robbed. All I know is that I came in here with several gold pieces and now they have gone.'

'I have only your word – the word of a man unable to find the price of a simple meal – that you have seen the sight of a gold piece in all your life. And as for being robbed, robbed by whom, may I ask? You are surely not suggesting that I—'

'All I am saying,' interrupted Amrach, 'is that I have been robbed. By whom I do not know. There were several folk in here when I entered and any one of them—'

'Several folk? Any one of them? You are quite mad, sir! You are the first customer I have had in here today. The weather has been foul and it is my sincere hope that business will pick up before nightfall – though little hope I have of that if those who do oblige me with their custom resist their responsibility to pay their dues.

'I tell you what I will do for you. I'm a fool to myself and I know it, but I like the look of that long leather pouch, empty though it is. With a generous heart I will take that in payment for your food. Now away with you before I change my mind and my good nature no long gets the better of me.'

There was little that Amrach could say in his own defence. For all the pouch was worth he decided that, in the circumstances, he may as well give it up. Having done so he left the inn, leapt astride his horse and rode off feeling greatly cheated.

'If the Paraclete always rides with me, then why did he allow me to get into that dreadful mess?' pondered Amrach as he reined Morning Breeze into a steadier gait.

'Because the Paraclete was not consulted about the matter,' came the immediate reply.

Embarrassed by the recollection that not even his most private thoughts were hidden from the Paraclete, and therefore not even from the Lion himself, Amrach sprung to his own defence.

'I spoke with you last night before I lay down to sleep.' His confidence grew as he considered what he thought to be the force of his argument. 'In fact, if you think of it, it was really not "last night" at all – it was the early part of today. So if you look at it that way we have already spoken.'

'Amrach,' said the Paraclete, 'if we are to speak only out of duty we may as well not speak at all. Our time together has little value if it is motivated by constraint. If you had consulted the mind of the Lion with regard to the path, you would not have been made an object of derision by the very people who attacked you.'

'But the other road was rougher and more harsh,' argued Amrach.

'And who told you that – the stranger? The one you met during the storm? And you trusted his word even though you did not know him and concluded that he was acting in your best interest? You must learn that little decisions often lead to great consequences and the doors of history move on small hinges. You would do well to consult the Lion for the direction of all your paths and not just delegate to him those things that appear too difficult for you.'

Amrach winced under the justifiable sting of the rebuke and attempted to parry the blow by diverting the conversation.

'Well at least the Silver Sceptre was not stolen – we can be thankful for that.'

'It was not stolen,' replied the Paraclete, 'because it cannot be stolen. It can never be taken from you by force. To relinquish it, and the responsibility that goes with it, you must lay it down by an act of your own will.'

'That I would never do,' said Amrach, sounding somewhat pious in the light of his recent failure.

'Make no rash promises,' replied the Paraclete. 'Pray only that you have the strength to hold on.'

'I will,' said Amrach, spurring on his horse as if in an attempt both to accelerate away from a sense of his disappointment of himself and of grieving the Paraclete.

By the time that Amrach had cleared the Chanuts valley, the sun was once more edging its way from behind the grey clouds and, as it did, Amrach too began to rise into a better spirit.

He turned his horse into the first village that he came to and was greeted by a group of small children, ragged and poor, who danced and laughed as they jostled around him.

'Does your horse have a name?' they asked him, pressing nearer.

'His name is Morning Breeze and you can stroke him, if you like. He will not bite, though you better watch out – if you stand too close he might tread on your toes.' At this they laughed and giggled all the more. Amrach, seeing that he was not going to make much more progress concluded that this might be a good place to dismount.

'Over here, sir, if you will.'

Amrach looked across to where the directions had come to find that it was a woman who had addressed him.

'Can I be of any assistance to you?' he asked the woman, who appeared to be in some distress.

'I would not bother a stranger normally, Sir, but there seems no one else around to help. Some fellows brought my husband to our door badly injured. He appears to be in a terrible state, Sir. They said that they found him beside the road and believe that he must have fallen from his horse. They have left him with me. Would it be too great an imposition to ask your help to carry him into the house and onto his bed?'

The man in question lay slumped and groaning at the entrance. His clothes were soaking wet and his long dark hair was straggled and matted across his unshaven face. Amrach lifted him as best he could and, with not a little effort, heaved him in the direction of the room from which the woman beckoned.

His outer clothing removed and hair towelled dry, Amrach suggested that the man's wife bring to the room some hot water. It did not appear that any bones had been broken, but the wound on the man's head gave every indication that his rescuers had been right in the assumption that he had fallen from some height and with a great deal of force, quite possibly from a horse. The water brought, Amrach, with the aid of a cloth, gently bathed and cleansed the area around the gash. That done, he left the man to rest.

'That is so kind of you Sir, we are very much in your debt,' said the woman. She handed Amrach some refreshment that she had made while he was tending to her husband.

Amrach was almost pleased, for once, to be in someone else's debt – especially after his encounter with

Darak and Berekah. He assured her that this had been no inconvenience and thanked her for the drink.

'You see we have only recently moved here to this village, just a matter of days in fact. Times have been extremely hard for us of late. Had it not been for the kindness of the owner of this house, allowing us the shelter of it for such a modest rent, who knows what we would have done? And now with my husband laid aside like this . . .'

Amrach could see that she was near to tears.

'I am convinced that he will get better soon,' he offered. 'There seem to be no bones broken, and though he may be sore for a few days, I am sure he will quickly regain his health.'

Amrach then went on to relate his recovery after what had happened to him on the Plains of Shephelah. The woman appeared to be comforted by all of this and said as much. Amrach rose to go but he thought it best to look into the small bedroom where the man was laying before he took his leave.

The man had regained consciousness and, as Amrach entered, waved him towards the wet clothes that lay in a heap upon the floor. As he lifted the sodden coat the man made a great effort to draw the garment towards him. His face showing some strain, he reached into a mud-stained pocket and handed to Amrach its contents. Amrach pressed four of the gold pieces back into the man's palm and would have taken none at all had he not noticed on one of the fingers that proffered them, a large gold ring.

7

The Teachers of Madon

Having sought and secured for himself accommodation in the village that he had since discovered was named Baqar, Amrach spent that night and the better part of the next day there.

Never before had he encountered a people who were so hungry for knowledge. Living as they did in the land of Phos they knew of the Lion – that is, they knew that his capital was the Stronghold of Theotes but that was about all. They had heard, however, of few of his exploits, and had even less knowledge of his present power. The Great Invisible One was totally unknown to them, and the same could be said of the person of the Paraclete.

Amrach made sure this time that he consulted the Paraclete as to whether it was appropriate for him to lengthen his stay at Baqar. He received his assurance that it was.

'No seeking heart shall ever be denied,' the Paraclete had said. 'No one who offers themselves in totality and with sincerity to the service of the Lion will ever be refused.'

'How far must I travel before I reach Madon?' Amrach enquired of one of the men from the village.

The man pointed to the brow of a hill eastward of where they were now standing.

'When you reach that point, you will see the village stretched out before you – although I suppose that it is the Palace that you really want.'

As Amrach rode off, he wondered why it was that he had not asked further about the Palace. Perhaps he had misheard the man, for what ruler would build his residence on the outskirts of such a small community of people?

It did not take him long to reach the brow of the hill. Just as he had been informed, the panorama before him embraced not only a medium sized village but also, on its perimeter, a large sandstone building which he assumed must be the palace in question.

Soon horse and rider reached Madon itself and, as he rode through it, he was struck by two remarkable things. The first was that almost everyone he saw was of middle age or older. The second was that, without exception, each inhabitant wore a coloured feather about his or her person. The feather was either red or yellow and was worn mostly on a coat lapel, though occasionally they were worn on a hat. He considered this to be most peculiar. But the most disconcerting thing of all was that, as he rode by, people eyed him up and down as if it was he, and not they, that were odd. In a way he was, if the definition of 'oddness' could be interpreted as riding featherless through a street. Had the Paraclete not made it absolutely clear that this should be one of his stops, Amrach would have been inclined to ride on and bypass Madon. But the instruction had been clear and, after all, he had travelled quite a distance to get there.

On seeing a refreshment house of some sort just off the main street, he decided that this should be where he would attempt to find out more details about this peculiar place. The establishment was empty of customers and in consequence someone came to take his order almost as soon as he had taken his seat.

'Not very busy today,' said Amrach to the servant girl as she approached him.

'Not just now, my dear – but we will be in a very short while. You chose a very good time to come. Mind you, when you hear the bell toll from the Palace tower there will be a real difference. Just you wait and see.'

'Strange place for a palace,' said Amrach to the girl. 'What is the name of the ruler who lives in such a magnificent building, but in such a remote place?'

'Oh, it's not a palace like that, my dear!' said the girl, with the kind of giggle that suggested that for once she was pleased to have access to information that someone else did not possess. 'It's a palace of learning. I thought everybody around here knew that.'

'Well I'm not from around here,' said Amrach, 'and I have to say that I have never heard of such a thing before.'

'Not heard of the Palace, dear? Well, just think of that! You must have come from a very long way away then.'

'I most certainly have,' said Amrach. 'Perhaps you could tell me about all these strange folk – the ones with the feathers.'

'Oh, they are the teachers, dear. They live in the village. The fact is that hardly anyone lives in the village but them.'

'Well then, where do the students live?' enquired Amrach.

'They live in the Palace of Learning itself, and only rarely visit the village. I am told that everything they need they can obtain within the Palace walls.'

'I see,' said Amrach, but just as he was about to enquire further he was interrupted by the ringing of a loud bell.

'Oh goodness, I'm going to be rushed off my feet now and no mistake. You just watch. I'd better take your order now. What would you like?'

Amrach placed his order, received his lunch and, just as the maid had said, within minutes the eating house was jammed. There were two spare seats at the table at which Amrach was sitting. Two men, both wearing feathers, were standing at the door, their eyes surveying the room and looking for a place to sit.

'Would you very much mind if we joined you?' they asked as they approached the precious benches. When Amrach smiled and waved his hand towards the seats, they sat down.

'We do not get many visitors in Madon at this time of year – we presume you are a visitor?'

'Yes, indeed.'

'And what is your business here?'

Amrach knew that the conversation would have to come to the matter in hand before long, but was somewhat startled that the issue was addressed so soon. It was almost as if a knife had cut short the pleasantries and small talk. He was taken aback.

'Well the fact is . . .'

The men eyed him intently:

'Yes – go on.'

'The fact is that I have come on an extremely important errand – commissioned by none other than the Lion himself – and I shall look to address the whole of Madon at some point, teachers and students alike.'

It was now the turn of the two teachers to be startled.

'I suppose that you are aware,' said the man to Amrach's left, 'that it is deemed a very great honour to speak to those who reside in the Palace of Learning. Our scholars are drawn from the very cream of the youth of Phos. They already know much about the Lion and, by the time that they finish here, will know a great deal more. I should also add that all of them expect to rise to some of the highest levels of administration in the land.'

'And furthermore,' interjected the one to his right, 'I hope you don't mind me being frank, but the privilege of addressing such noble minds is not put at the disposal of every passing stranger.'

'Then how does one go about addressing these "noble minds"?' asked Amrach, a little disappointed in himself that he had allowed a trace of sarcasm to add a cutting edge to his response.

'One does not go about it at all,' said the man to his right. 'One is invited, or one does not speak.'

'I see,' said Amrach, and in an attempt to diffuse the increasing sense of tension in the conversation he parried the latest verbal assault with another question.

'Perhaps you would be willing to explain to this stranger the significance of the feathers? I notice that they come in two colours.'

The two men in an identical reflex looked down at their lapels with a thin-lipped smile of pride.

'They actually come in four colours, but it is likely that you will have come across only two. The red feather denotes our qualification to teach "The History of the Lion".'

'And the yellow feather?' asked Amrach.

'The yellow feather,' answered the other, 'displays a person's right to teach on "The Current Edicts of the Lion".'

'So because I do not have a feather, I cannot speak?'

'You understand exactly!' they answered simultaneously and smugly.

For a moment Amrach was distracted. He could not help but notice that the servant girl was alone and that people were calling her from all directions at once. He saw her pick up two heavy jugs in her hand and, for a fleeting moment, wondered about the contents. Was it water, wine, milk or mead? As the girl made her way towards those who had placed the order, negotiating a path through packages and assorted feet, she stumbled. The earthenware vessels fell from her hands, crashing to the ground. The contents of wine burst over the occupants of nearby tables to the unsympathetic cheers of a large proportion of the clientele.

'You are not listening to a word we are saying to you, are you?'

'Oh, I'm sorry,' said Amrach, returning from his distraction. 'Yes, I think I understood you. You said I could not speak unless I possessed your coloured feathers. And that's the end of the matter is it?'

'Yes, we are afraid it is.'

'And that situation obtains even though I carry the Lion's Silver Sceptre?'

'You have the Silver Sceptre?' they chorused with united incredulity.

'I most certainly do,' said Amrach, his confidence now accelerating.

'Well, that does put something of a different complexion on the matter. What I suggest is that we relay this conversation to our superiors, and speak to you again on this issue as soon as we can. I think that we could go so far as to say that, if we could prevail on you to meet us here in perhaps two hours time, we may well be in a position to clarify the matter for you.'

Amrach found their new attitude helpful and told them as much. He took the opportunity to take a stroll and, true to their word, his meal companions returned precisely at the appointed time.

'And how did you fare?' asked Amrach as the three of them resumed their seats.

'Our superiors were most interested that one had come to Madon with the Lion's Silver Sceptre,' ventured the first. 'But they say that before you can be allowed to address the Palace of Learning, it is essential that you first oblige them with your presence at the Conclave.'

'And what precisely does that mean?'

'It precisely means . . .' the man continued, rejoicing in the fact that their featherless stranger was not to be allowed unhindered access to the palace. 'It precisely means that after the ringing of the evening bell you will be asked to proceed to the main entrance. You will then leave your name with the Palace steward and expect to be taken in due course to the oak chambers.'

When Amrach arrived at the chambers he discovered them to be aptly named. Access was via two large oak doors and, once inside, all the walls were panelled with wood of the same variety. At the far end of the room was a long table that stretched for the most of its width. Behind the table, and facing Amrach, were seven men. They were different in bearing and appearance but all, without exception, wore on their lapels two feathers – one red and one yellow.

All the chairs were of the same size except the one in the middle which was larger than the rest, and on which sat a man with sallow complexion and pinched features. He had a melancholic expression and proceeded to drum his fingers on the table. Amrach was drawn to the conclusion that he had not wanted this meeting to be convened in the first place, and was anxious for it to be over even before it had begun.

Amrach had no sooner got his bearings when someone signalled for him to sit and an attendant moved forward with a chair.

'This meeting has been called because we understand that you wish to address the residents of the Palace of

Learning,' the chairman began with some indifference. But before he could continue, one of their number interrupted by saying:

'This is all so unnecessary! The man has no feathers and that is the end of it.'

'But he does have a Silver Sceptre,' offered another.

Amrach looked round and his gaze fell upon the latest speaker, a kindly man who continued:

'If Amrach—I believe your name is Amrach, is it not?'

'Yes, indeed.'

'If Amrach has a mandate from the Lion, then surely we are completely out of place to even question whether he addresses us. On the contrary, we should do all in our power to assist him.'

'Sceptre or not,' the melancholic man retorted, 'we have a duty to question him on the content of his message and he must submit himself to our interrogation.'

When Amrach informed them that he was more than happy to respond to any questions that they may wish to proffer they eased themselves back on their seats as he made his introduction. He told them of the reason for his visit to Phos. He made it clear that he was there to raise an army and that he expected volunteers to come from among those who were residents of the Palace.

'I think the whole matter is an irritation, a bother and a nuisance,' said the melancholic man the moment that Amrach had finished.

'And what is more,' he continued, 'I consider it to be singularly inconsiderate of him to impose himself upon us disrupting and disturbing the focus of our scholars with talk of war. It is most inappropriate – I might add, exceedingly inappropriate.'

The kindly man rejoined the debate.

'Given that we now know the nature of your visit and the proposed content of your message, I feel that it is important that you be allowed to address us, whether we agree with you or not.'

'But the feathers, the feathers – what of the feathers?' cried another.

'And anyway, where do you stand on the roast duck issue?'

'I beg your pardon,' said Amrach. 'I thought you said the roast duck issue.'

'That's exactly what he said,' offered another member of the group. 'Do you presume to lecture us and are ignorant of an issue of such importance as that?'

Amrach nearly laughed out loud, and summoned every nerve to stop himself from doing so. The kindly man threw his quill pen onto the parchment in front of him and leant back in his chair, obviously exasperated with his colleagues for raising the point. It was clear that the questioner considered this to be something of very great importance; his head was strained forward and his eyes fixed on Amrach, awaiting his response.

'I have to confess,' said Amrach with a note of incredulity in his voice, 'that I am totally ignorant of the roast duck issue and find myself unable to make any intelligent reply on the matter. Perhaps someone could assist me and then I may be in a position to offer an opinion.'

The kindly man had now retaken his quill and, with smiling eyes that signalled a measure of sympathy to Amrach, explained:

'Around three hundred years ago there was an earthquake in this region that devastated the area on which the Palace of Learning and adjacent village now stands. Shortly before the calamity, it is said that a large flock of ducks flew overhead and made a great deal of noise as they circled what was then the old village. The people ran out of their houses and cottages to witness this strange phenomenon and eventually the ducks flew away from the area. In consequence the people followed the direction in which they had gone. Once they were out of the village, the earthquake struck and all the dwellings were levelled to the ground.'

At this juncture Amrach noticed that the melancholic man was amongst those who held linen handkerchiefs to their eyes, obviously overcome by hearing this evocative story. He then turned his attention back to the speaker who continued.

'Although all their possessions were lost, their lives at least had been saved. Of course the details are not clear, because with the passing of time—'

'The passing of time?' interrupted the melancholic man angrily. 'What you are saying is bordering on blasphemy. There is no question about the matter!' he argued, choking back a sob.

'Well,' continued the speaker unabashed, 'tradition has it that this took place on the first Wednesday in the month. So on the first Wednesday of each month, right up until the present day, the inhabitants of the town eat roast duck in gratitude.'

Amrach thought it highly inappropriate – not least to the ducks – to celebrate in this way, but considered it best to keep his thoughts to himself.

'And the feathers . . . ?' asked Amrach, as if picking up the final piece of a jigsaw.

'You have grasped the point exactly,' said the kindly man with a wry smile. 'Seeing that the ducks had brought knowledge of the impending disaster, it was decided some years later to build the Palace of Learning on the site. The feathers that are worn on our lapels are duck feathers.'

'I see,' said Amrach. 'But how is this an issue on which I am asked to express an opinion?'

'The issue,' said the melancholic man sternly, 'is that there are some among us who have the arrogance to suggest that roast duck may be eaten on any day during the first week rather than on the designated Wednesday. Others say that the tradition need be observed only once a year and – I can hardly bring myself to say it – there are those who say that it need not be remembered at all. They have the temerity to say that our historic traditions take our eyes off the Lion himself, but the ducks . . . the ducks . . . the ducks!'

He had now completely broken down and appeared absolutely inconsolable.

Others recounted that this controversy had spread to the residents of the Palace of Learning and was perhaps the major topic of debate. Though they were not yet qualified to wear feathers of red or of yellow, their lapels or hats were adorned with white or green depending on their position.

As Amrach considered the magnitude of the subject that had brought him to the Madon, and the threat posed by the Princes of Harag, the argument of the consumption of roast duck would have been laughable beyond belief were it not so desperately sad. He began to feel emotions rising in him bordering on an anger that he hoped was righteous. Long before he had come to Phos, he and his wife had taught their children about the primary truths that centred on the Lion, the Paraclete and the Invisible One. They had often discussed how each related to the other and, most especially, of the necessity of understanding their decrees and the importance of doing their will. It was now time, he felt, for him to speak.

'May I ask you all a question?' asked Amrach.

The oak chambers fell silent; few had assumed that any questions might be directed to them.

'Proceed then,' said the chairman, reluctantly.

'Are any of you familiar with the village of Baqar?'

'Of course we are. It is a village adjacent to our own and has the privilege of being the closest of the surrounding communities to this great Palace of Learning.'

'Well, I stopped off at that village on my way here and found the people to be gracious and warm but with little knowledge of the Lion and his ways. When I began to tell them of his greatness and his power it was all that I could do to get away, so hungry were they to hear more. I found it strange that, as you have pointed out to me the proximity of the Palace to the village, so much knowledge should reside next to so much ignorance. Are you not aware of this? And, if so, what steps are you taking to remedy the matter?'

'And who do you suggest should break into their busy schedule to do this?' asked another of the seven indignantly.

'Well, I suppose those who are the most qualified,' said Amrach. 'The residents of the Palace must surely have some responsibility, but may I suggest that the onus rests largely on you?'

The meeting degenerated into an uproar. Amrach sat as a spectator as they argued among themselves. Some were saying that the visitor was right and that they were remiss; others were arguing that that whole notion was ridiculous. This went on for some considerable time and with such ferocity that it was clear that they had forgotten that Amrach was still there.

Correcting this oversight, Amrach was then asked to leave the room while they conducted their discussion in private. After the steward had led him to the door and seated him in adjacent room, Amrach was still able to hear the raucous debate. Not even the panelled walls were able to muffle the sound. A casual observer may have concluded that that there were seventy in the room rather than seven.

'I wonder what the Lion would think about this,' thought Amrach.

'The Lion knows everything about this,' responded the Paraclete. 'One of the reasons he has sent you here is to stir the cauldron of their hearts. Some think that the primary purpose of the Lion is to bring peace throughout Phos. There are times, and this is one of them, when he must agitate the waters within the hearts of men. It is often only then that what lies in the heart's depths is disturbed, and that that which lies in darkness rises to the surface. Do you remember the incident in the eating house?'

'You mean my conversation with the two teachers?'

'No,' said the Paraclete. 'What occurred when the servant girl was carrying the earthenware jugs. Do you remember wondering what they contained?'

'I do indeed,' replied Amrach, 'and those who sat nearby soon found out to their dismay.'

'Sometimes,' said the Paraclete, 'you never know what people are carrying inside until they are upset. The Lion has other centres of learning throughout the land of Phos. Many of his subjects, men and women, young and old are preparing themselves. They are like arrows in a quiver seeking to be ready for the moment when the hand of the Lion is upon them and he places them in his bow. The Lion's heart is towards this place. There are those among the number with whom you met who are being disturbed. You have been sent to trouble the waters. Wait and see Amrach, wait and see.'

To his surprise Amrach was granted permission to speak to the residents of the Palace, and on the very next day, he took his place on the platform of their magnificent assembly hall. Many hundreds of pairs of eyes locked in on him from the long body of the auditorium, as well as from every corner of the three great galleries. They gazed in wonder on him: not because of his stature or his looks, but because they saw that his lapels were devoid of feathers.

It was the member of the interviewing panel who had acted kindly towards him that had been elected to introduce him. Perhaps, Amrach thought, no one else had been willing to take the responsibility upon them. Mention was made of the Silver Sceptre, and at that, there was such a gasp that Amrach thought he might be sucked towards the centre of the hall, so great seemed the intake of air!

There was no doubt that he had a captive audience. No one so much as stirred as he recounted the purpose of his divine errand. Many hundreds of young men and women sat transfixed as he shared with them his vision. Drawing to a close Amrach said:

'And so I end what I have to say by asking this question: in the light of what I have told you, what do you perceive to be your highest priority, what is your noblest goal? You have heard of the Roast Duck controversy upon which you are all so divided. But I would have you look, not three hundred years backwards, but rather to this present day and the vital days that are to come. I would have you consider a real battle and a contemporary threat – to look to something that concerns not our yesterdays, but is vital for our tomorrows. I call upon you to rise with me against the Princes of Harag in the power and authority of the Lion. To fight, to fight and to fight again until the victory is ours. The Lion calls for us not to split hairs, but to release captives!'

At this, all the young people in the Palace rose to their feet cheering and shouting, 'All Hail the Lion! All Hail the Lion!'

They had given the greatest possible assent to the challenge that Amrach had brought before them. Some began to pull the feathers from their lapels, and once this was started, it was taken up by them all. Feathers of white and green cascading like coloured snowflakes whispered downwards from the balconies and, as members of the Conclave ushered Amrach out through a back door, they could hear as they left a rousing chant that grew in intensity, 'From the past into the future!'

'They are calling for you to address them again,' said one of the Conclave, 'and I have to say that I think that it would be best – if only to bring them to some degree of order.'

Compliantly, Amrach retraced his steps to the stage. There was great cheering and applause when he reappeared and, standing before them with hands raised, motioned for them to be silent.

'It is good to be stirred,' began Amrach. 'It is right to allow our feelings to rise in anger against the arrogance of the Princes of Harag but more, much more, is required of us. It is essential that we mobilise. Talking of war has never once inflicted so much as a bruise upon the enemy, let alone defeated him. My mission is taking me to other locations around the land of Phos. But be assured of this – I shall return. I shall be back for you: until then, continue with your studies. It is important that you are sharpened in mind as well as in spirit. The Lion is also concerned about the toning of your intellect. We need to be fully equipped for the challenge – body, soul and spirit. In the same way that the Silver Sceptre was entrusted to me so, if you follow me, the Sceptre shall be become yours also. I say to you farewell . . . but only for a time!'

Amrach had spoken with the intention of calming the uproar, but the sounds that now met his ears caused the previous tumult to pale into insignificance. Yet he knew as he left that he had not left chaos behind him. The first cries had been the swirling waters of raw energy; this was something different. His mind soared back to the Blacksmith's forge and he pictured the red heat of metal upon the anvil. These were not uncontrolled and destructive flames. Something was being welded into the resolve of these new warriors. Something was being harnessed among the furore that was about to create an avenue for change. Amrach, inspired by the Paraclete, had provided a framework through which this passion could be channelled. The residents of the Palace had lived too long in the arid and dry desert of intellectual debate. These cries were expressing their gratitude for unexpected rain.

As he left the palace area, Amrach was approached by a burly figure who introduced himself by the name of Qatsir.

'A most inspiring address if I may say so, Sir. And also – if I may make so bold and if you would not think that I was presuming too much – I would be more than willing to er, gather these enthusiastic people together – under your banner of course Sir – to await your return to us.'

Amrach was uneasy at the nature of the man's approach. He had come to learn over the years that those who spoke most at length of the need of humility were often the most proud, and those that regaled their followers on the need for submission often did so because they wished to live and act as lords. However, in the belief that there was little harm in this, and without consulting the Paraclete, he gave Qatsir his permission. He would learn of his mistake not many days later.

8

The Cave in the Wilderness

On the morning of the following day Amrach spoke with the Paraclete.

'To think,' said Amrach, 'that I recoiled from visiting a "mere village". If I had not been obedient to the will of the Lion then all the events of the past few days could not have occurred. This has taught me a salutary lesson.'

'You have been able to learn that, while you see only time, the Council of Theotes views time and eternity simultaneously,' the Paraclete responded. 'Too many mortals think our vision is as limited as their own and consequently miss out on so much that could be theirs if only they could learn to trust.

'The next phase of your mission is to take you to the furthest extremity of the land of Phos, to a town called Masas. In order to reach it you will need to travel over a great deal of rough and rocky terrain. It cannot be reached by any other route and, in consequence, has few visitors. It is the will of the Lion that you make your way there with haste. The watchmen who man the towers of the Stronghold of Theotes have received intelligence that the Princes of Harag are marshalling their forces and it is anticipated that they will begin their march in just a few weeks.'

Amrach and the Paraclete talked for some time longer. Amrach asked many questions and the Paraclete, in response, offered Amrach much encouragement. He was given clear directions as to the way that he should take to the town of Masas and so took careful note of the places that he must pass through in order to reach it.

He had not travelled very far before both he and his horse became aware of the changing landscape of the countryside. Lush pasture and green meadow gave way all too suddenly to harder ground and rougher passage – just as the Paraclete had warned. Amrach had more than once been thankful to Berekah for giving him such a good mount as Morning Breeze. He found that his horse could negotiate all but the most difficult terrain. The two of them had become good companions along the way.

As the quality of the paths grew worse so did the weather. It was not just the rain but the thunder and lightning that accompanied it that convinced Amrach that he should look for shelter as soon as he could. No dwelling places of any description were in sight and few trees grew tall enough in this area of boulders and stones to offer any sanctuary from the elements. To his right, on higher ground from where he was, he imagined that he could see what looked like a cave and so turned his horse off the narrow path and headed towards it.

As he drew nearer he was able to confirm that it was a cave. The mouth of it proved so large that both he and Morning Breeze were able to ride into the entrance without the need to dismount. He was little concerned as to where the cave led, if in fact it led anywhere at all. His only thought was that he and his animal might secure some shelter from the powerful and raging storm. The sky had darkened to such a degree that it was only by the flashes of lightning that he could make out the contours of the road that they had only recently vacated. Amrach took off his cape and, having shaken the surface water from it, looked round for somewhere to sit. He concluded that they might be there for some time to come.

'Would you care to join me for a little bread and cheese?' spoke a voice from the deeper darkness of the cave.

Startled, and not for a moment expecting to find another living soul in this inhospitable climate, Amrach's eyes searched for some sign of movement. A figure came towards them and, as he did, Morning Breeze took a few nervous steps back as if uncertain as to whether safety lay in the teeming rain or the proximity of the advancing sound.

'I'm sorry if I alarmed you, but there are few ways of making an introduction in a dark cave without causing at least a measure of anxiety. In fact, when I saw you enter I stood back for a little while, unsure as to how I might commence a conversation without frightening you.'

The owner of the voice was now visible. He seemed at first to be an old man – the long unkempt beard gave that immediate impression. However, as Amrach looked more closely it was evident that the man could not have been more than forty years of age. His clothes were not so much ragged as well worn, and although his manner was pleasing and unthreatening, Amrach noticed a dullness and sadness about his eyes.

'So we have both chosen the same spot to shelter,' he said, thinking of a way to respond and not wanting to offend the man by revealing the degree to which he had been alarmed by his approach.

'This is my shelter, though not only in the storm. This is my home. I live here,' the man replied.

'You must forgive me,' said Amrach. 'It had not been my intention to intrude. I had no way of knowing; it was just to get out of this awful downpour, you understand.'

'Oh, think nothing of it. How should you know? And, in any event, I do not own the cave – I simply live here.'

Amrach introduced himself, but gave the man no information either of where he had come from or the name of his destination. The man in return said little of himself, other than to say that he was called Zohah.

'Could we have possibly met before?' asked Amrach. 'It's just that your name seems familiar. While it is an unusual name I am quite certain that this is not the first time that I have heard it.'

Zohah assured Amrach that it was not at all possible that they had met, as he seldom wandered far from the cave and had lived there for a number of years. The man lit a torch and by its light constructed a fire. Though Amrach's eyes had become adjusted to the darkness, it was not until the slender red fingers of flickering light illuminated the contoured walls of the cave that he noticed the large portions of meat suspended from its roof.

They dined and chatted for the remainder of the day as the storm gave no indication of blowing itself out. Though they talked at length, by the time they settled down to sleep Amrach was no clearer about the man's identity and was still troubled by the familiarity of his name. He was absolutely convinced that he had heard it before.

Amrach awoke early the following morning to speak with the Paraclete. He rose, not because of piety, but because of the hardness of the cave's floor. Animal hides that Zohah had given him for a bed had done little to lessen his discomfort. He ventured out of the cavern and found that, although it was still dark, the rain at least had cleared. Filling his lungs with fresh morning air, he pushed back his shoulders and stretched himself into a new day.

'I am troubled by the name, Zohah,' said Amrach to the Paraclete. 'I know I have heard the name before, but I just cannot place it.'

'Think back to the Stronghold of Theotes. If you remember, when you entered you asked your friend Darak about those whom you saw surrounding the Lion's throne. He pointed to the Commanders –'

'That's it!' exclaimed Amrach. 'On one side of Lion stood the Daughters of Zohah – I knew I had heard the name before. But perhaps this is a coincidence. This cannot be the Zohah of whom we speak – the father of those who are privileged to abide so close to the Lion himself.'

'This is Zohah, poor Zohah.'

'But how can the Lion allow a man to live in such poverty?' Amrach asked.

'I speak of poverty of spirit, not poverty of material resources,' replied the Paraclete. 'I shall not tell you everything; let Zohah speak for himself if he wishes, but I will tell you this – the man you see over there still sleeping on a bed of skins was once one of the noblest men in the Stronghold of Theotes. He was a powerful man. His five daughters grew up under his good influence and became like him in many ways. They became mighty before the Lion, and such was their influence that they became known as the Prophetesses of Theotes. This was not a title that they took upon themselves. This was a reputation that they had gleaned through always accurately relating the mind of the Council of Theotes to the subjects of the land.

'On many occasions Zohah carried the Lion's sceptre and travelled the length and breadth of the land of Phos in the Lion's name and with his full authority – just as you are doing. On one such mission he was ambushed by some infamous enemies of Theotes. You will, I am sure, not be unfamiliar with them.'

'The bloodline of Harag,' offered Amrach briskly, indicating to the Paraclete that, though he had guessed, he wanted him to continue with the story.

'Precisely. The details of the trap that they laid for him I need not go into but, as a result of this encounter, Zohah failed in his mission and in consequence was forced to lay down the Sceptre.'

'So he ran here in disgrace,' conjectured Amrach, 'unable to face those he had once served?'

'No, it was not like that at all. Zohah returned to the Stronghold and spoke of his failure before the Council of Theotes. Nothing of all that had taken place did he withhold from them and furthermore, he asked that any punishment that they designed might be such that his failure might be redeemed. You are aware, I presume, of the great doctrine of the 'Transformation of the Lion'? asked the Paraclete before being willing to continue the story.

'I know that once, the Lion was a Lamb,' said Amrach. 'I am aware too that the Invisible One was angry at the wickedness of the land and was about to destroy it. I know that the Lamb offered to take the whole punishment of the land upon himself, though he had done no wrong. And everyone is aware that the Invisible One agreed to this.'

'You are correct,' said the Paraclete. 'The Lamb died but was later resurrected as a Lion. From that time onwards, all who submitted themselves to the Lion received the forgiveness of the Invisible One. However, all who refused his forgiveness would be called upon to submit themselves eternally to their deserved judgement upon their death.'

'I have understood this since a child,' said Amrach, 'and know too that, though the Lamb was changed in appearance to the form of a Lion, he never lost the heart of a Lamb. His nature never changed. When a Lamb he had a Lion's heart and when a Lion he had a Lamb's heart.'

'Well,' continued the Paraclete, 'because Zohah was truly repentant and did not try to hide his failure from the Council of Theotes, he received forgiveness. True, the Silver Sceptre that was lost from his grasp he was not able to regain but, once his strength was rebuilt over the passage of time, there would have been other missions and other sceptres for him to carry.'

'Then why does he live here, all alone, in this cave?'

'He hides here,' said the Paraclete. 'Because even though the Lion has forgiven him, he cannot forgive himself. This is true of many mortals and not least of Zohah.'

'Forgive me for asking,' interrupted Amrach, 'but why did you not speak to him? You are, after all, one of the Council of Theotes. Surely you must have gone with him on his missions in the same way that you accompany me?'

'I have tried many times to speak with him. Yet each time he has resisted me.'

'Resisted you!' retorted Amrach incredulously, 'How can anyone resist you?'

'Think back to the Valley of Chanuts, Amrach. When you did not consult with me with regard to the road that you should take, did I force the will of the Lion upon you? I think not. I long to speak again with Zohah and to have him in fellowship with me – but such a thing must be in his heart as well as in mine.'

Zohah stirred from his sleep. Thinking that Amrach was simply admiring the view, and not aware that he was talking to the Paraclete, he came across and joined him at the mouth of the cave.

'So which way will you go from here?' enquired
Zohah as he drew alongside.

Amrach turned towards Zohah, and as he did so their
eyes met. Zohah had been on enough missions, and spoken with the Paraclete so many times himself, to know
that Amrach was no ordinary traveller. He sensed that
there was something about him that indicated that only
moments ago he had been in the presence of one of the
Council of Theotes.

Zohah swung back round towards the darkness of the
cave and Amrach turned round too. Amrach put his
hand on Zohah's shoulder, desperately hoping that a
touch would communicate a whole vocabulary of
words. But as Amrach made this gesture Zohah pulled
even further away.

'Why have you come here? Why do you hound me?
Cannot I be left alone? You have been sent from the
Stronghold and I know it. Go away and leave me in
peace.'

And with these and other protestations Zohah did all
that he could to distance himself from every overture of
Amrach's brotherly concern.

'Zohah, I know now who you are. The Paraclete has
revealed it to me. But believe me that was not the case
when I entered the cave yesterday. It was only when I
talked with him in the early hours of this morning that I
discovered your real identity.'

'Well now you know. Go on your way. You presum-
ably know who I was and you know now who I am.
Now leave me to myself and go!'

'Yes, Zohah I do know who you are – a man mighty in
the power of the Lion: a man who accomplished many
missions and someone who, like me, has carried the
Silver Sceptre in the Lion's name: a man who was
mighty then and can be mighty yet. You are also, Zohah,

a man who has raised five daughters who stand this very day in the presence of the Lion at the Stronghold of Theotes.'

'Don't talk about them to me,' shouted Zohah, swinging fiercely round this time to face Amrach. 'Do not speak of those who once looked upon me with pride and now remember my name only in shame. Bring not before me the perpetual reminder of my sin. Leave me as I am, I implore you. Leave me alone and be gone.'

'Oh yes – I will talk to you of your daughters. I knew yesterday, as soon as you told me your name, that I had heard it before. Let me tell you this Zohah, and listen carefully as I speak. The ones known as the Prophetesses of Theotes no longer allow themselves to be called by that name.'

'I thought as much,' sobbed Zohah as he buried his face in his hands. His voice was partially muffled as he continued. 'It is just as I said. Not only am I ruined – I have also ruined them, the ones who stood in the Great Hall. They who went from there to bring comfort to the needy; my daughters are ruined – and not for any crime that they have done, save that they are my offspring.'

'Wait, Zohah, wait. You know not of what you speak. Your daughters still stand there. The reason why they will not allow themselves to be called the Prophetesses of Theotes is because they wish only to be called the Daughters of Zohah. I was there myself at the Stronghold not many days ago. I saw them for myself. It is in that name that they were pointed out to me, and I will tell you the reason – look at me as I speak!'

Zohah was crouched on the ground, his head still buried in his hands, but Amrach, reaching down, encouraged him to lift his tear-stained face towards him.

'The reason,' Amrach continued softly, 'is because, even before they wished to be known as the

Prophetesses of Theotes, denoting their calling – they wished to be known as Daughters of Zohah, your children – offspring of their father. Their love for you, and their faith in you, is so strong that they yet believe that you will return to the Stronghold and stand with them in service of the Great and Mighty Three.

'Listen, Zohah – I know how heavy the Sceptre can be. Its weight can feel almost unbearable at times. You have been on many missions and I on only one, yet I am not unaware of its great responsibility. You are wasted in this cave. This is not the place for you.'

Zohah got to his feet, walked once more to the mouth of the cave and looked out over the rocky terrain before him.

'I have often longed to go back, but not because I missed the prestige of the Stronghold or the importance of those missions. True, there were times when I longed to feel the weight of the Silver Sceptre on my back. But more than anything else I missed fellowship with the Council of Theotes – to see the Lion once again, to know the encouragement of the Paraclete and the overshadowing of the Invisible One. Oh how I have longed for it!'

Amrach drew again to his side and this time Zohah did not recoil from him.

'Then why don't the two of us call out to the Lion and tell him this?' suggested Amrach.

'I am willing,' said Zohah, 'if you believe that he will grace me once again with his presence.'

At this there was a sound of a rushing wind – not the destructive and wild forces that had driven Amrach to the cave but a powerful and positive energy that filled the whole area where they stood. And with the wind came a voice.

'It is I, Zohah – the Paraclete. I have listened to your conversation with Amrach. I have watched your every

step since the first day you entered here. I have never left
your side. Not for one moment have you ever left my
sight and my ear was tuned to your every whispered
cry. Though you did not call upon me, I cared for you
still. If you are willing to return you will find ready
acceptance. No one will be more pleased than the Lion
to see your face again.'

'I am overwhelmed,' said Zohah. 'Though undeserv-
ing of anything but judgement I will make my way back
to the Stronghold. I look not for reinstatement to the
position I once held – only for restoration to the man I
once was.'

'That is well said,' responded the Paraclete. 'And, if
Amrach is willing, I would like you to travel with him to
the place that I have prepared to be the next stage upon
his mission. That accomplished, I shall make preparation for you to return.'

'There is nothing I would like more,' said Amrach
reassuringly. 'We will make ready to leave at once and,
just think; if I had not been driven by the elements to
take refuge in this cave then this reconciliation may not
have come to pass.'

'Do not presume,' said the Paraclete, 'that the Lion
leads his subjects only through the gentlest paths. The
Lion can make even the storm become his servant and
the harsh wind to be his slave – that he might bring
every purpose to fulfilment.'

Amrach stood speechless before the Paraclete. Of
course, this had all been within the Lion's plan. He
and Zohah embraced one another as brothers and set
out together from the cave. Amrach unhitched his
horse while Zohah gathered together a few belongings
and some provisions for their journey. As they only
had one horse between them, they decided that it
would be better for them – and for Morning Breeze –

to walk for a while and allow the animal to saunter by their side.

They must have travelled for several miles before they reached the next inn and yet, if you could have asked them, they would have said it was little more than a stroll. Zohah was thrilled to be setting out on a new chapter of his life and Amrach had not realised how much he had missed the companionship of friends, until that joy was awakened by the fellowship of Zohah.

Although they had supplies with them, they thought it best to take food and drink and, if possible, to secure a second horse. They were able to fulfil both these objectives at the inn and, this done, they made their way onwards.

9

The Town of Maggephah

Amrach and Zohah had been informed while at the inn
that their destination, the town of Masas was still quite
some distance away. It would therefore be sensible to try
and find somewhere to stay for the night as it was
impossible to reach the place before dark.

The stones and rocks over which the two horses had
to pick their way made their progress slow, but they
were thankful that now at least the weather was good
and showed little sign of changing.

Their path took them through a small copse of trees,
and when they emerged on the other side and had travelled just a little way beyond, they saw three men
coming towards them on foot. Each was shouting and
waving their arms as they ran. Amrach and Zohah imagined they would run right up to them but they stopped,
as if at some imaginary barrier, and called across the gap
to them.

'Get back to the place from which you have come!
Return! Be gone!'

Their eyes were wild but with what appeared to be
fear rather than rage. It was now Amrach's turn to shout
across the distance that separated them.

'We have travelled far and desire to reach Masas.
What is your reason for barring our way?'

'It is for your own good Sirs, we assure you. To reach
the town of Masas you must travel through the town of
Maggephah.'

'Then let us pass through!' demanded Zohah, urging
his horse forward.

'You cannot, Sirs. We abide in the town of Maggephah
and it is ravaged by a plague, a dreadful plague. Many
are already dead and many more are dying. Those that
are left have reconciled themselves to an inevitable fate.
We are sent out to warn all travellers upon this road.
There is no other way into Masas so please Sirs, for your
own good, turn back!'

Amrach and Zohah looked at one another across their
horses.

'It is strange,' said Amrach, 'that the Paraclete did not
inform us of this. He would surely have been aware of
this dreadful calamity.'

'It is easy to see that this is your first mission,' replied
Zohah. 'It is my view that the Paraclete is testing us. He
is allowing us to discover a solution for ourselves – to
observe what we will do in such a situation.'

'I believe you to be right and furthermore I am convinced, for my part, what our course should be. I say
that we go on Zohah – what say you?'

'I am sure that that is right. We have been commissioned to go to Masas and, until we are instructed oth-
erwise, it is to Masas that we should go. It is evident that
the Lion has some design in this. We must learn to trust,
we must go on.'

The three men had stayed in their place assuming
that, their responsibility over, the two riders would turn
their horses round and accelerate as fast as they could in
the opposite direction.

'We have talked the matter through and wish to proceed. Please let us pass.'

'It is madness, Sirs! Believe us when we say you are taking a sentence of death upon yourselves. Why die with us? Return and live!'

'We are resolved to pass through,' Amrach called out. 'Please do not hinder us.'

They met the stench of Maggephah long before they entered the town. The smell of death was everywhere as were bodies upon carts. The marks made over the door ways of houses and cottages gave stark intelligence of the presence of the plague. As they rode on they heard the cries of the sick mingled with the sobs of the mourning. Wherever they looked, spelled out in a multitude of ways were the words, 'No Hope'.

The two riders arrived at a place where the two main roads that crossed the town met. At this junction stood a hall which appeared to be the centre of local administration. The edifice must have been used for ceremonial purposes and the principal gathering place of the people in better times. Today it stood like a dark monument to the pestilence and had been commandeered as a makeshift morgue.

As they continued they found long rows of unburied dead. In the same area the dying were receiving the best, but inadequate, assistance that could be found for them. A man, weary with fatigue and overwork approached to enquire what their business was. Instinctively the two companions racked their brains for a viable reply and then Zohah said:

'We have come from the Lion to rescue you from this plague.'

Amrach could not believe what Zohah had just said. It was evident that the many long months in the isolation of the cave had affected his mind. He instinctively backed away both from Zohah and the attendant as if, by doing so, he was distancing himself from the outrageous statement. He sidled away on the pretence of examining more closely an inscription on a nearby stone pillar.

'What on earth does Zohah think that he is doing?' thought Amrach in exasperation. 'The man is mad, he has to be. My mission is to raise an army – not attend the sick and dying and bury the dead. I have no skills for this and, as far as I am aware, neither has he. It was the will of the Paraclete that we pass through this place unharmed to reach Masas, not remain here inviting the plague to swallow us up with the rest of these poor and wretched souls.'

As these and similar thoughts somersaulted through his mind, the voice of the Paraclete broke in:

'Listen carefully to what Zohah will say to you. Do not rebuke him. Do not discourage him and offer him no arguments.'

'But—!'

'And offer me no arguments, either.'

At this point Zohah came across and joined Amrach at the pillar. His face radiated enthusiasm as he said excitedly,

'I have told the man there is nothing more to fear.'

Amrach swallowed hard.

'I have informed him that this very night, all who are able to do so should come and meet us here and we will pronounce their deliverance in the mighty name of the Lion. So – what do you think?'

The broad smile on his face anticipated a similar fervency from Amrach.

'What do I think . . . ?'

Amrach was aware that it was not only Zohah who awaited his response. The Paraclete was also listening.

'I think . . . that is I am sure . . . you must be right.'

Zohah put his hand on Amrach's shoulder and ushered him into the street with the air of one who expected nothing less from his friend.

'What exactly are the arrangements that have been made? What precisely did you say to the man in the Town Hall?'

'It appears that each night a bell is rung to summon the people in order that a tally might be taken of those who have died, and instructions given to them of the proper care for the sick. Tonight however, as the people gather, they will be told to bring the dying at the sound of a second bell. And that,' said Zohah, 'is when we shall introduce ourselves.'

They spent the remainder of the day, at least until the sounding of the first bell, trying to take in the full scale of devastation that the plague had inflicted on this stricken community. They watched as those still living passed by them, summoned by the bell's toll. Faces, hollow and jaundiced, and frames that were gaunt and thin struggled along the lanes towards the hall.

Amrach realised that at that very moment the exhausted attendant would probably be relating to the assembly the details of his encounter with Zohah. Every instinct in his body and brain encouraged him to run and hide. They walked on together and, while in no way wishing to contravene the commands of the Paraclete, he thought it in order at least to ask Zohah how long he had possessed the power to heal. He was filled with a sensation that bordered on terror when he heard Zohah's response.

'Heal? I have no power to heal!'

'Then what will you say to the dying that will confront you within the hour?' begged Amrach.

'I will say nothing, Amrach – you will.'

'I – what can I say? It was not me that made these arrangements, but you!' He wanted to say 'outrageous arrangements', but knew that the Paraclete was in attendance. 'It was you that offered that exhausted fellow hope. It is your words that are being relayed to the sick who have gathered, even while we speak. And you tell me that it is I that must confront these people – I who have never professed to possess any power to heal.'

'But you carry the Silver Sceptre,' said Zohah softly.

'The Silver Sceptre,' said Amrach pronouncing each syllable with deliberation and in a volume a little too loud for grace. 'The Silver Sceptre was entrusted to me by the Lion with respect to my mission to raise an army, and that is all. Nothing was said about humiliation, theft, rough roads, storms, plagues and pestilences!'

Amrach was inwardly ashamed of other thoughts that percolated through his mind. He would not dream of articulating them, but they were there nevertheless. It would have been all too easy for him to remind Zohah that it was not too long ago that he had been hiding in a cave, isolated and cocooned from the real world. He bit his tongue and was glad he did, for in the depth of his soul he was well aware that this was not the issue. Zohah was a forgiven man and had been so for many years. He was not about to do him the disservice of undermining his new found confidence and trust. The real issue, and Amrach in his most honest moments knew it, was that Zohah's faith in the Lion's power served as an indictment on his own lack of assurance and trust.

The ringing of the second bell interrupted any further introspection and the two of them made their way back to the hall at the centre of Maggephah.

'I have explained to the people only that they are to be addressed by two strangers who have travelled from the

other side of Phos, and it is now open to you to say to
them what you will,' invited the weary attendant.

Without any more ado Amrach, having found a vantage point from which most, if not all, could see him,
prepared himself to speak. Looking out over a crowd
ravaged by disease, he began:

'Friends, some time ago I stood in another hall just as
I stand here today. It was the Great Hall at the
Stronghold of Theotes and I was in the presence of the
Lion. It was a memorable moment and the day on which
I was given the Silver Sceptre. It was then that I received
the commission to travel throughout the land and raise
an army to defeat our enemies, the Princes of Harag. The
Lion entrusted the Sceptre to me with these words, "Go
in my name and with my authority!"

'In the days that have followed I have endeavoured
faithfully to fulfil the trust that the Council of Theotes,
the Mighty Three, have placed in me. I and my companion Zohah stand before you today because, in our different ways, we have experienced first hand the evil that is
perpetrated by the enemies of Phos. Though we have
faced numerous trials, and in them at times experienced
personal failure, never once has the Great Council of
Theotes failed us.

'We have learned during this time two life-giving
principles. The first is that as mortal men we are as weak
as the Mighty Three are strong. We would have you
know, and be in no doubt, that we do not stand before
you in our own power or name. The second is this – all
destructive forces of violence, error and disease are alien
to the Lion, the Paraclete and the Great Invisible One.'

And then Amrach did something that he had never at
any point in his mission done before. Though he had
often made mention of the Sceptre, never once had he
revealed it to those to whom he spoke: not to Darak, not

to Zohah, not to anyone. He took the Sceptre that had been slung across his back and, having unwrapped it, raised it high above his head:

'Look on this, people of Maggephah. Fix your gaze upon the Lion's Silver Sceptre. Rivet your attention upon its form: not as an idol that is elevated above you, but as a symbol of the Lion's power and all that is inherent in his name.'

Shouting and loud cries came from the body of the hall as from the Silver Sceptre there shot forth beams of fire and of light. Amrach and Zohah, as stunned as the citizens themselves, watched as those who lifted their eyes towards the Sceptre were made the targets of its rays. As soon as a cowering and diseased body was touched by its force, the person's form became enveloped in its glow and, from within the mantle of its light, they emerged healthy and whole.

Amrach said nothing more, nor could he. The two of them continued to watch as miracle after miracle took place. When Amrach's arms grew tired through holding the Sceptre aloft, Zohah supported them with his.

Not until all had been healed did Amrach remove it from their sight and into its covering. Everyone gathered within the hall examined with disbelief their transformed bodies, and then, as soon as the truth had dawned, turned to rejoice ecstatically with those around them.

'All hail Amrach! All hail Zohah! All hail the great Sceptre!' the crowd cried out.

'Stop, Stop!' pleaded Amrach, as he again reminded those who thronged the hall that what was happening was solely due to the Lion's might and power.

'All hail the Lion! All hail the Mighty Three!' became the new anthem chorused by the crowd.

'All hail the Lion, indeed!' said Amrach to the people. 'You must remember this day not just as the time of the turning away of the plague, but as the occasion of the Lion's intervention. Always keep before you the fact that, in matters large and small, the Lion longs to intervene on your behalf. Endeavour daily to reverence the Council of Theotes in your hearts and within your homes. Never again allow defeat and hopelessness to cloud the prospect of the Lion's power.'

Instructed by the Paraclete, Amrach and Zohah stayed in Maggephah for the next few days. They visited homes and instructed many in the ways of the Mighty Three and from that town conscripted many – especially those who had been miraculously healed, into the Lion's army. This having been done, they made their way in the direction of the place that had originally been their destination: the town of Masas.

The first lodgings where they stayed outside Maggephah were comfortable. It had been a strenuous though exciting few days and when they retired both of them slept soundly. But during the night Amrach experienced a strange and terrifying dream.

He found himself transported into a great banqueting hall in which much feasting was taking place. The tables were laden with the choicest food and all who dined were robed in the finest clothes. Their manners were as impeccable as their conversation was sophisticated and Amrach concluded that he was among people of great wealth who lacked for little, if for anything at all. It was plain that there was far more food and provisions than there were guests. Amrach made this point to the person sitting next to him.

'What will you do with all the provisions left over after the feasting has ended?' he asked.

'Discard it. What else?' was the reply that was given, and given in such a way as to suggest that the question had hardly been worth the bother of asking.

'And furthermore,' the person in the adjacent seat continued, 'we will do the same with all the plates, bowls and goblets too.'

'You mean you will set aside these ornate, beautifully patterned dishes to be used at a later date, perhaps on some other feast day?'

'Not at all – we shall discard them in case we should become bored with their appearance.'

'Is that not a terrible waste?' said Amrach in disbelief.

'What is waste when you have plenty? After all food is only food and dishes only dishes, are they not? But enough of this; may I take the opportunity to introduce you to my wife?'

Amrach nodded in polite recognition towards an attractive woman who was evidently many years younger than her husband. Not until then did Amrach notice that every man in the banqueting hall had a partner with him that appeared considerably more youthful than himself. It was evident that the man did not seem to think it strange that Amrach was there without a partner, nor even that he was there at all.

Amrach was then transported from the brightly lit environment in which the vision had begun, to the stark contrast of the cold fields outside. He looked back to the place where the feasting was taking place, which appeared to him to be several hundred yards away. Yellow light cascaded through its windows, penetrating like bright spears into the deep blackness of the night.

He turned away from his view of the building on hearing the noise of what sounded like iron upon iron. It was hard to distinguish precisely what it was. All he could really be sure of was that the noise was about as far from him in one direction as the hall was in the other and that it was coming ever closer. His eyes adjusting themselves to the darkness, he was able to make out a column of advancing children and, as they neared, the sound became recognisable. It was the sound of chains. To his horror, he saw small children shackled the one to the other and, in turn, to their captors.

The cruel column rattled past him and Amrach was aghast at the anguished and terrified faces of the infants. Each turned their head as they travelled by as if in some macabre salute. As their eyes momentarily engaged his own they seemed to shout an entire vocabulary of words, but their lips only mouthed what appeared to be a silent scream.

'Let them go! Let them go!' Amrach cried to the captors as the long line straggled past.

He watched the faces of those who held them at their mercy. Some laughed and mocked, others hung their heads in shame – guilt written large upon their countenances.

'Release them, please! Please let them live! Allow them life!'

In response the captor's hollow call rang back:

'Disposable . . . Disposable . . . Disposable.'

The long line reached the hall, passed within yards of the muffled sound of its revelling and travelled on into the deeper darkness of the night. If rage and compassion ever met, they met in Amrach's voice as he called out after them once more:

'Please let them live! They should not die!'

Yet it was far too late for that, and with that cry upon his lips he awoke from his slumber.

10

The Children of Nasham

The following morning Amrach and Zohah began their day by speaking as usual with the Paraclete and, instruction and encouragement received, continued on their journey to Masas.

'What a nightmare I had last night!' said Amrach as their two horses trotted side by side.'What haunting images appeared before me – scenes that, though I would long to erase them from my mind, I fear that I will never be able to forget.'

'What did you see?'

Amrach described the dream. The vision seemed as vivid as when he first received it. He was surprised that he was able to remember every detail, from facial expressions to the sound of the chains. Having finished he asked his companion what he thought of the dreadful spectacle.

Zohah paused for a moment before replying. Eventually, as if forced to reveal some deep mystery that would have been better left hidden, he answered with a strange reticence:

'You have been permitted to witness the horrendous plight of the Children of Nasham.'

'Children of Nasham?' enquired Amrach. 'Surely that name means "Children of Destruction". Was this more than a dream? Were these children really about to be slaughtered? And, what is more, how do you know about them and their fearful predicament?'

'One question at a time,' said Zohah, raising his hand as if trying to withstand a flood that was about to engulf him.

'There is something I have not told you – something that needs to be said. Perhaps it is right for you to know that I have been to the town to which we are travelling on a previous occasion. It was several years ago. From what you have related of your dream it is clear that the Paraclete has granted you a vision to prepare you for what lies ahead.'

'You have been to Masas before, and you never told me?' said Amrach, surprised.

'Perhaps I should explain. Around twelve years ago I carried the Lion's sceptre to this very place. Intelligence had come to us at the Stronghold that there was a community of people living on the perimeter of the land of Phos that was experiencing much hardship and deprivation. Year after year the harvest had either been of poor quality, or else there had been none at all. My assignment was to travel with the Paraclete and seek to lift the people from the poverty that was engulfing them.'

'Surely the Lion could have lifted them from poverty to plenty with just a word?' said Amrach.

'He could have done so had he wished, but it was not as simple as that. Many years earlier the area had known much prosperity, but they and their leaders had entered into practices of great wickedness. As a result of the evil in which they were involved, they brought a judgement of famine upon themselves. There is a day in all our lives,' said Zohah with some feeling, 'when we must sit down to a Banquet of Consequences. But let me continue.

'I was commissioned by the Lion to call upon them to change their ways in order that they and their families could live once more without the fear of pestilence hanging above their heads. However, they refused to hear the message that we brought even though we told them that it could free them from their awful plight.'

'They chose poverty? I can hardly believe that,' said Amrach.

"They chose poverty,' confirmed Zohah.

'When I addressed the people I was shouted down and, when I insisted on speaking, I was physically thrown out of the town.'

As Amrach listened, his thoughts went back to his experiences at Chaneph and with a knowing sigh, bade Zohah to continue.

'Eventually their plight worsened to the point that death and sickness ravaged the land. Some time later, knowledge reached us that that there were individuals, just a small number we were told, who were now ready and willing to repent of their shameful ways and return to the Lion's rule but, mark you, there were only a few. The Lion decreed that he would once more attempt to communicate with them. He longed that they might return to him so that deliverance could be theirs. The ones that were chosen to go this time were the Prophetesses of Theotes.'

'Your own daughters?' exclaimed Amrach.

'Yes, my own daughters.'

For a few moments their conversation was interrupted as both endeavoured to encourage their horses to negotiate a path that, already strewn with rocks and stones, had now begun to climb much more steeply.

Once their mounts had regained some momentum, Zohah continued.

'Some of the Lion's Commanders argued against the plan, and for two entirely separate reasons. The first was that as I, their father, had been physically thrown out of Masas, what danger might the womenfolk have to face? The Lion countered this by reminding his Commanders that his designs, whether in prosperity or adversity, depended not on whether his servants were men or women, old or young, weak or strong. His followers were secure because he made them so.

'The second argument that was put forward was based on the fact that there were so few, from the reports that had reached us, that had given any indication of a willingness to return to the teaching of the Lion that it was hardly worth the risk or trouble. After all, they argued, Masas was on the farthest edges of the kingdom. No one offered any more objections after they heard the Lion roar, "I will send my servants to the opposite side of my universe if it means the salvation of one life".'

'I am sure that that put a swift end to the matter,' said Amrach.

'You can be sure that it did.'

No one was happier than the horses to reach the summit of the hill, and no one more amazed than Amrach at the panoramic view that stretched out before them.

'Surely that is not Masas?' he said to Zohah in a tone that clearly reflected his bewilderment. 'Not those fine buildings which give every indication of opulence and wealth?'

Zohah had given his assurance that it was, and as there was still some distance to travel before the town was reached, he continued with his story.

'The reason that my daughters were chosen to travel to Masas was because it was known throughout the land that they carried with them the gift of prophecy. It was understood that they would not go with their own words, but would speak only that which was given them by the Lion through the power of the Paraclete.

'They went through the town speaking words of warning to those who remained stubbornly set against turning from their destructive path, and words of encouragement to those that were open to repentance. Those that chose to forsake wickedness received forgiveness and, when my daughters were driven from the land, they too were expelled.

'When the people were challenged as to why they would not listen they excused themselves by retorting that they had nothing to learn from the lips of women.'

'It never occurred to them I suppose,' said Amrach, 'that the importance was not the messenger whoever he or she might be, but the message.'

'No – this was merely a device to convince themselves that they could remain entrenched in their shameful ways. Nor did it occur to them that the messengers had come with the Lion's mandate.'

'All this I understand,' said Amrach as they approached the town, 'but this is no poverty-stricken community, and you have not yet mentioned those that I saw within my dream, those that you referred to as the Children of Nasham.'

'I will come to that presently. Shortly after my daughters were driven out, other messengers came: not this time from the Stronghold of Theotes, but from the Princes of Harag.'

'The Princes of Harag have also been this way before?' gasped Amrach.

'Not the Princes themselves, but their emissaries. It is important to understand that all the evil perpetrated within Phos, as well as outside its borders, emanates from them. I can assure you that though their armies have not yet entered, you can be sure that their spies are everywhere – passing on intelligence and planning their incursion. It is in their interest, and it is their highest priority, to turn the people from the Lion's ways. Their main weapons are discord and disunity and they seek to sow such evil seeds wherever they can.

'Anyway, Amrach, lest you take me further from my point, let me return to my account of the messenger that came from the Princes of Harag those years ago.

'They came not only with words but with gifts, lavish gifts. They praised the people of Masas for standing out for so long against the Lion, and promised to reward them further. In short, they gave the people everything they asked for. Nothing of material substance was withheld. Their engineers rebuilt the town and bestowed great wealth upon the people.

'Because of this its citizens began to openly mock the Lion and his followers. They said that, if by their wickedness they had brought a curse upon themselves, then it was clear that by their own efforts they had rid themselves of all afflictions. Pointing to their affluence, they declared that no longer had they either need or reason to fear the Council of Theotes. Others went so far as to teach that the very existence of the Lion was a myth. After all, they said, "Bring out any man or woman who has ever seen him!" '

The sign that informed them that Masas had been reached stood to their left as they rode by.

'But this still does not explain my dream,' said Amrach. 'What of the Children of Nasham?'

'They built these great edifices – these large and ornate buildings that we are now approaching. They wanted for nothing, and yet as a consequence of their growing greed, were never satisfied. Teachers rose among them that encouraged them to dismiss the very idea of "right and wrong". They became like mariners without fixed points upon their compass, tossed about on the waves with neither rudder or sail. But to them, that did not matter as they had no path to follow other than the fickle inclinations of their own desires. They said that they did not consider themselves to be lost, for they are only lost who know from where they came, where they then were and the place to which they are travelling. Their own words condemned them.

'Their feelings became their only guide and, as their feelings changed, so did their laws. Things that their leaders abhorred one day they embraced the next. Their only rule became what they 'wanted' and the only crime became the existence of anything that they did not want.

'Their possessions they changed the moment they ceased to be fashionable. Those married, where marriage still existed, discarded their partners as soon as they grew tired of them or felt that they had grown too old. Children too were seen as the "possession" of the women and if these were found inconvenient these too became disposable.'

'Disposable!' exclaimed Amrach, 'That was the word in my dream – it was the very horror of its sound that woke me from my sleep. Those that I saw must have been the Children of Nasham. Can it be true that these were being marched off in their chains to be slaughtered?'

'What you saw,' said Zohah, 'were only spectres – symbols if you like – of those who died before they came to birth.'

By now they were well into the town and, as they rode along, there was every indication that they were in a community that possessed everything that money could buy. Amrach reined in his horse and brought it to a standstill.

'It's no use,' he said, 'I shall have to return. There is no way that, having heard what you have told me, that I can spend a moment longer in this vile place. I will travel back or even go elsewhere, whatever the Paraclete wishes, but I cannot stay here.'

'The Paraclete has already clearly expressed his wishes to you,' Zohah said. 'He has conveyed to you the will of the Lion. The Council of Theotes has decreed that you should be in Masas.'

'There is no point. What good would it do? They have rejected the message twice already. What purpose would be served by communicating with a people who have been infested with the philosophy of Harag? It is a town that stands in blatant opposition to everything that we are fighting for and which nurses at the very breast of our enemies!'

Though Amrach could not be induced to go on, he was persuaded not to return until they had communed with the Paraclete. He forcefully restated his case but the Paraclete was adamant.

'I notice a serious stubbornness in you, Amrach,' the Paraclete said. 'How long will it be before you are the messenger and not the message? It is for you to deliver it as it is given not edit it as you see fit. You are called to convey the message to those to whom it has been sent, with a servant heart.

'Do not suppose,' the Paraclete continued, 'that the miracles that took place before the people of Maggephah gives you some importance because it happened that it was you who held the Silver Sceptre in your hand. Look at your hands. Are they not ordinary? It is the Sceptre through which the Lion's power flowed that turned back the plague. You have authority, but it only has credence as you go in his name, with his message to those to whom he chooses to send you. Should you decide to go in your name, and with your own message, to a people other than those to whom you are directed: then you stand before the world as a mere mortal and nothing more.'

These were by far the hardest words that Amrach had ever heard from the Paraclete since the first day that his assignment had begun. What affected him most was the fact that what he was hearing was something that he had been told, in different ways, many times before. Deep inside he longed for new insights. Now he was beginning to realise that he was having great difficulty in remembering, and holding on to, the old lessons. Trusting was proving hard. One thing that he was sure of was that the Paraclete would never use a weapon that would wound him. The sharpness of the instrument he now felt upon his soul was surely nothing less than a surgeon's knife – wielded only to bring him health.

They continued into the town. Zohah had listened to all that the Paraclete had said and so thought it best not to intrude into Amrach's thoughts. The two rode on for a while in silence.

11

The Incident at Masas

They dismounted their horses at the town square and set out to find a place to eat. Having dined well, they decided to take a stroll.

Amrach wondered how a town of such beauty could mask so decadent a reality. Manicured lawns, flowered terraces, ornate ironwork were all in abundance.

'Does one of you gentlemen go by the name of Amrach, may I ask?' said an immaculately dressed man as he approached them.

'That is indeed my name, but how would you know it? I have only just arrived and have never been to Masas before.'

'Be that as it may,' said the stranger. 'However, I would be obliged if you would come with me, and your friend as well of course.'

He beckoned them to a smart carriage drawn by two glossy-coated chestnut horses.

'You are on foot, I see,' said the man as he opened the carriage door with an indication that he wanted them to enter.

'We left our mounts at the town square,' said Amrach, 'but we are more concerned as to the reason for your approach. To my knowledge we have not met before and, if we have, then you have the advantage of us.'

'You are not the only man to whom the Paraclete speaks. I do not wish to make a great point of it, but it would not be wise for the three of us to be seen together and, if you would be so kind . . .'

The man's right hand was on the handle of the open carriage door and his left hand made a gesture toward the opening which suggested that the three of them should enter quickly.

Seated, the stranger gave two sharp taps to the carriage roof and, that acting as a cue, the coachmen called upon his horses to proceed.

'You must forgive what must appear to be an uncivil introduction to you gentlemen. My name is Ragal. You I know to be Amrach, and you Sir . . . ?'

'My name is Zohah.'

'Not the Zohah whose daughters . . . ?'

Not wanting him to continue lest unpleasant memories be evinced, Zohah interrupted the man and confirmed that he was the man whose daughters had come to Masas those years before.

'It is a great pleasure to meet you, Zohah. Your daughters were very brave and we owe a very great deal to them, I assure you.'

'I appreciate what you are saying, and thank you,' said Zohah. 'But please tell us why you have taken all this trouble to meet us today.'

'Well, as I have said, my name is Ragal. I have lived in Masas all my life and was born into a family that suffered much hardship and great poverty. I was still a young man when your daughters came to Masas and can remember only that they brought an unpopular message and that they were thrown out, together with the small numbers that were impressed by them.

'When the emissaries from Harag came to the town it became clear that, though much affluence had come into Masas, the quality of life had continued to deteriorate. It was hardly noticeable at first but then evil was stacked upon evil. It was during this time that I began to enquire more closely as to the content of the message brought from the Stronghold. Though its substance was always conveyed to me in terms of mockery, it was not too long before I was able to piece together the basic themes. After a while I became totally convinced of its truth and wondered whether I, like the rest, should leave Masas and head for the Stronghold.

'During those days when I was considering what I should do, I was awakened during the night. The windows crashed open under the pressure of a mighty wind which swirled around the room. To begin with I was greatly afraid. A voice spoke, which later I was to learn was that of the Paraclete himself. I was of course amazed that he should want to communicate with me.

'He told me that I should not be fearful and, at this assurance, I began to feel my misgivings slowly subside. I was astonished by the revelation that he knew all about me: my past, my struggle, my desire to investigate truth and my present state. He went on to say that those who had left had done so at the Lion's command. It was as right that they should leave as it was that I should stay. He told me that I should remain resolute and wait until two strangers should come to the town, one of which would be carrying a Silver Sceptre and that his name would be Amrach.'

'Hold on,' said Amrach, wide-eyed. 'Did you say that this happened years ago?'

'I did,' replied Ragal.

'But that was long before I set out on my mission, years before the Lion was ever known to me.'

The carriage lurched and swayed as the chestnut horses turned a sharp corner at speed. Zohah smiled and said to Amrach:

'The Lion may not have been known to you, but you were certainly known to the Lion. He knew you not only before you were married, but before you were born.'

'Before I was born?'

'Of course – not only known, but also he designed that one day you would be carrying his message around the land of Thos.'

'I find this remarkable. It seems strange to be engaged in supernatural encounters such as we have seen and yet feel so under-qualified for my role. I need to be constantly learning in order to grow further into the Lion's purpose. But, enough about me – go on, Ragal, with your story.'

'The Paraclete said I was not to speak too openly of my recently-discovered knowledge as there would be time enough for that in the future. So, from that time on, I communed regularly with the Paraclete. And it was only a few days ago that he informed of the immanence of your arrival.'

At this point both horse and conversation came to a standstill.

'I believe we are here now,' Ragal said.

There was a shuffling noise as the coachman stepped down from his seat and opened the door for the three of them to step out. Amrach and Zohah found themselves standing at the gateway of a large house and, as Ragal led the way to it, they both presumed it to be his. On entering they saw, even from the vantage point of the lobby, that it was sumptuously furnished. Tall doors opened onto large rooms and servants scuttled about their business while butlers and footmen crossed the marbled floors at a more sedate pace.

'I know what you must be thinking,' said Ragal. 'How can I live in such elegance without compromising my position as a follower of the Lion? Is that not what is in your mind?'

It was exactly what was in Amrach's mind, but he said nothing.

'There is nothing wrong in having possessions,' said Zohah. 'A difficulty only arises if the means of their acquisition compromises integrity. Possessions must never abdicate their servant role. We must possess them. They must not possess us.'

Amrach thought that he was being unnecessarily eloquent, but considered the thought well put.

'I can put you fully at your ease in this regard,' said Ragal. 'My work within Masas calls upon me to oversee all our planning regulations and, while extremely well paid for my work, involves me in nothing that could cast dishonour or discredit upon the truths I now hold dear. My home is at your disposal while you are here and all that I own is yours should you require it.'

'Do you have a family?' enquired Zohah.

'I have no family at all. My parents both died some years ago and I never married.'

'And what of friends?' asked Amrach.

'I have many acquaintances, but few friends. Were people to know the views that I hold I would have none at all. It would have been much easier over the years to flee to the Stronghold but, as the Paraclete once told me, that would be an escape rather than a refuge, so I have stayed. You may not realise it, but you are the first people of a like mind with whom I have been able to speak in confidence that I have met since the Paraclete first made his presence known to me.'

'It is good to meet you,' said Amrach, warmly shaking his hands. 'The sacrifice that you have made is immense.

But please go on – we were only told that we should come to Masas and nothing more. Are you any wiser than we are about the next steps we should be taking?'

'I am indeed,' Ragal replied. 'And I have to tell you that this point in your mission will be the most perilous that you have encountered so far. Listen to what I have to say next with great care.

'There can of course be no question of you being invited to address any of the large town meetings for, as soon as anyone of influence finds out your identity, all access to the population will be denied to you and you will both be arrested.'

'Then how are we to proceed?' asked Zohah.

'Each night of the week, most of the people of the town attend the Coliseum of Joy – a place of, well I use the word "entertainment" advisedly. Neither you nor I would call it that. It is a vile place – an arena of deca- dence and cruelty. But such is the mentality of Masas that everything is turned upon its head. Evil is enter- taining, to be perverted is to be popular and to be lewd is to be liked.'

'After what I have learned about this place nothing would surprise me. Yet what has the Coliseum of Joy got to do with our task?'

'Let me explain further. In the middle of the proceed- ings there is an interlude. One of the employees of the Coliseum will make an announcement with regard to the things that are planned for the audience's pleasure during the remainder of the week. As soon as that is done the people retire for refreshment before returning to their seats for the remainder of the performance.'

'I still don't follow,' Zohah said.

'What I have arranged,' continued Ragal, 'is that you, Amrach, take the place of the announcer in this evening's performance.'

There was a time, Amrach thought, when he would have protested. But by now he had learned that it was useless. He knew that, whatever he said, the Paraclete would have an answer. He thought back again to something that had been said to him early in his assignment that 'when our will crosses the Lion's will, our will must die.' As a guardian of the Remnant Legend his life had been continually in danger. He thought of the price that his wife had already paid and dare hardly go on to think of what was happening to his sons – if in fact they were still alive. Whatever he would say to Zohah and Ragal, he knew deep down he would do anything they asked.

'I have orchestrated, and it is not necessary for you to know how at this juncture, for you to stand in his place at the conclusion of the first half. No introduction is expected and so no one will be surprised when you take up your position. The tradition is that the announcer is in costume and masked – so you will be safe at least until you speak.'

'Until I speak,' echoed Amrach with irony. 'Well that's a comfort!'

'You will I am sure understand that it is vital that you do all that you can to convey your message as quickly and succinctly as possible. Who knows what the reaction will be?'

'Ragal is right,' said Zohah, 'What better opportunity would you have to speak to so many?'

'That is easy for you to say,' said Amrach, 'It is not you who are going to have to stand up before this mob. It is I!'

'Well, I said it was going to be dangerous, did I not?' interrupted Ragal. 'If you feel unable to proceed with this plan then that, of course, is a matter for you.'

All three of them were to be found that night in the wings of the stage at the Coliseum of Joy. Amrach had thought that nothing would surprise him, but the opening half of the night was to prove him terribly wrong. The sights that he witnessed were an attack on everything that he knew to be true. It was an assault on his mind and all of his senses.

A moment before he was due on stage the Paraclete drew alongside him.

'Amrach, you have reached a most strategic point in your mission. Up to this time you have been on the defensive. Now is your time to attack. Your message here is not about raising an army and of summoning warriors to your side. Tonight you are declaring war! Tonight you are giving those who follow the Princes of Harag notice that the Lion is marshalling an army. They have heard time and time again the message of the Lion that they should repent of their ways. Each time they have ridiculed and mocked his messenger. Over and over again they have been told of his gentleness. Tonight they are to hear of his awesome authority. This day you will give the Powers of Darkness notice that the Lion is for war and that all the Princes of Harag are destined for defeat. Go in the Lion's name Amrach. Go!'

In that instant there was no place in the universe that Amrach would rather have been. He felt that at this moment he was in the centre of the Lion's will as never before. As he moved to the centre of the stage and looked across the leering faces, his thoughts were filled with images of his brutalised and dying wife, the enslavement of his sons, the plague-ridden people of Maggephah and the screams of the helpless and enslaved Children of Nasham.

He spoke as he had never spoken before. For a while the audience listened in a stunned state of shock, in disbelief at what their ears were hearing. Then the full force of the message began to envelop them. It was as if all the evil in the universe was gathered in a single place. Their eyes seethed with violence as their voices screeched obscenities.

When the uproar was at its height a ferocious wind swept through the place, dreadful in its fury. Burning torches that illuminated the Coliseum collapsed and fell from their high and ornate plinths, plummeting to the ground showering sparks and flames and igniting everything in their proximity. Everything not fixed to the ground swirled around as in the violent vortex of a whirlpool. As the fires undermined the masonry, sections of the roof fell like giant hailstones to the floor below.

In the mêlée and confusion Amrach, Zohah and Ragal made their way back to the house.

'Once the chaos and commotion calms down,' said Zohah, 'people may suspect that you had a hand in this, Ragal. They will be calling for your blood in the same way that they did for Amrach's. Now is the time for you to leave. Your job has been done and you must come with us.'

'The Paraclete has already informed me that, once Amrach had delivered his message, I was indeed at liberty to leave. So, if I have your permission, I would like to come with you.'

'We would be delighted to have you join us,' said Amrach, 'and if you will be so good as to secure yourself a horse, and show us the way from here to the town square where we can take possession of our own mounts, we will be on our way. Who could have known, only a few hours earlier as we sat here, what amazing events the night would unfold.'

'You most probably would have entered into another argument with the Paraclete as to why you should not be obedient to the Lion's will,' said Zohah, smiling as he took his friend's arm and ushered him towards the door.

'Is that so?' replied Amrach. 'Then perhaps you are in danger of underestimating me. We are all climbing. The tests may well be growing harder, but we are also becoming stronger.'

'You may well be right, Amrach, you may well be right,' apologised Zohah.

And the three of them advanced out into the darkness.

12

The Warrior Named Qatsir

The three men thought it wise to put as much distance as possible between them and the town of Masas and so, in consequence, rode throughout the night. They need not have been over-anxious. Had they consulted the Paraclete on the matter, they would have discovered that nothing could have harmed them for there was yet much work to be done and their mission was by no means yet accomplished.

As day dawned they drew aside from the path and rested; all three of them entered a deep sleep from which they emerged invigorated and refreshed.

When the Paraclete was consulted he informed Amrach that the part of the mission in which he was commissioned – to call the land of Phos to arms – had now come to an end.

'It may be,' the Paraclete suggested, 'that you are surprised that this part of your assignment is so soon accomplished, with visits to so few towns and cities having been made. What you will not be aware of is that, while you have been moving from place to place in obedience to the Lion, much has been happening in the places that you have been.

'The next stage in your mission is to return to the areas that you have visited and, when you have done that, to march with your army to the Stronghold of Theotes. As for Zohah and Ragal, they are not to accompany you. They are to make their way directly to the Stronghold by a shorter route and you will be reunited with them later. The Daughters of Zohah already know of their father's return and there is already much rejoicing.'

'Do you not mean,' interrupted Amrach, 'that there will be rejoicing when they see their father?'

'I meant exactly what I said. The Daughters of Zohah rejoice as if their father was already there for, though they do not see him yet, they believe my words. You see they have learned to trust.'

Amrach wished he had never opened his mouth.

The three parted company not with sorrow but with joy as they knew that they would meet again before too long.

Zohah was glad not to be returning to the Stronghold unaccompanied. Ragal had a great deal to catch up on; there was so much that he had wanted to know and learn, and what better teacher could he have than Zohah?

Amrach had a tumultuous welcome in Maggephah. The town was almost unrecognisable. He could hardly believe the transformation that had taken place in just a few short days. Radiant faces met him everywhere he went and a banquet was held that night in his honour.

Entering the Town Hall, which on his first visit had been the scene of scattered bodies wasted by the plague, he was welcomed by a man who embraced him with enthusiasm.

'What a joy to meet you again – what a blessing that you came! You have brought the town alive again. It has been resurrected from the dead and no mistake. How long will you stay? What are your needs? Is there anything that we can do?'

Amrach took in little of what he said. He wondered who the man was, although his face seemed vaguely familiar. And then he recognised him – it was the person that he and Zohah had once described as the 'weary man'.

'Where is Zohah? Is everything well with him?'

'Yes, Zohah is well. He has gone to the Stronghold of Theotes and I shall see him later.'

'That is good,' said the man. 'And now, to the Banquet! 'You will, I am sure, be willing to speak to us before the night ends?'

'I will be glad to if you wish,' said Amrach as he was directed to the top table.

Music, singing and dancing filled the night with rapturous celebration. Amrach could not help but compare this with the scenes that he had witnessed at the Coliseum of Joy. What he witnessed here was a real and lasting happiness – a joy of a durable kind.

The meal over, it was time for him to make his speech and he rose to much applause. When it had died down he began:

'Good friends, more has taken place in my life in the past few weeks than I could ever relate to you in the time at my disposal. One thing I will say is this; we are living in great and momentous days and even better times are ahead of us.'

Once more applause rose from the attentive crowd as Amrach continued:

'You have given me a great welcome and I thank you for it; but I beg you not to forget the words that I spoke as I stood here on the day I held the Silver Sceptre before you. Remember, good citizens of Maggephah, that it was not my power that accomplished this. It was the Lion's work. Use your new-found health in service of the Lion. Expend your strength at his behest. I have known great men who in their suffering have risen high to do the Lion's will. What then do you consider is required of you – those who have been recipients of his goodness and his grace?

'I am leaving here tomorrow. I trust I will not go alone. There is great rejoicing here, and rightly so, but these sounds must not block out too easily the cries of those who yet languish under the cruel heels of the Princes of Harag. I call for troops to join my side. I look for leaders among you who will rise for battle. I ask for lives to be laid down in total surrender to the Lion's will!'

Amrach's words evoked a great response and many folk rose to the challenge. He signalled for silence once more, and then he continued:

'But before I sit down I will say one more thing. I was asked what honour I would like to receive, or what gifts I would wish for myself. I look for neither. I ask but for one thing. I ask that from this day the name of this town be changed from Maggephah, meaning plague, to Rapha, which means healing.'

The cheers of affirmation that followed left Amrach in no doubt that his request had been granted, and the next day he left Rapha with a great crowd of warriors accompanying him.

Progress was slower now that there were so many people on the roads and this, combined with the rocky terrain, retarded their headway even more. At one point along the way Amrach, who was leading the long procession, raised his hand for the column to come to a standstill.

'We are pausing here for a while,' he shouted, straining to project his voice as far as he could. He watched as the people looked around for a reason why they were being asked to stop, there of all places. There was no shade or shelter, no water hole or pasture – but nevertheless they obeyed. Those upon horses dismounted, and those on foot sought out accommodating boulders on which to take some rest. Amrach had stopped because he wanted to visit, one last time, the cave in which Zohah had spent the past long years in solitude and isolation.

It was not until he had almost climbed to its entrance that he realised that he had been followed by two of the leaders of Rapha. They had assumed, it seemed, that he had seen something suspicious and they wanted to be by his side in case he was exposed to any danger. There was little point, Amrach thought, in bidding them return – even though he wanted to be alone.

He looked into the mouth of the cave. It was not enveloped in a dark storm as it had been on the first occasion he stood there, but nevertheless his eyes still needed time to get used to the dark. Slowly, familiar things came into view: the pots and pans, the cold charcoal remains of a spent fire and meat long past its best suspended from the roof. Amrach sank quietly to his knees and bowed in silent thanksgiving to the Lion that Zohah had been delivered from this place.

The silent men looked on and then one asked:

'Did a holy man live here?'

'Yes,' said Amrach, 'a holy man lived here.' And, as they descended the slopes to join the rest, they wondered why his eyes had grown so moist.

They journeyed on until they reached the outskirts of Madon. Amrach had forgotten that, although he had been there before, this was the first time that the majority of those that followed him had ever set eyes upon the Palace of Learning. He realised this when someone asked the very question that he had once posed:

'What kind of ruler would live on the outskirts of a village?'

He inwardly smiled as he gave them the very answers that had been given to him when he had first come upon the town.

When Ragal had left his house in Masas he did not do so before taking with him every gold piece he had saved during his past years of prosperity. He surrendered these to Amrach for the maintenance of the army for as long as the money would last. Amrach handed some of the coins to one of the leaders whom he had designated the Quartermaster. Then he, and a small group of his men, rode into Madon itself.

Amrach decided to go directly to the Palace of Learning. His men waited outside as he made his way through the tall doors. The steward recognised him instantly and Amrach enquired as to whether or not it would be convenient to speak with the Conclave.

The steward went to investigate this possibility and, in due course, returned to say that access to the Conclave could not be granted at this time. When Amrach asked if he could make an appointment for some period in the future, possibly the next day, the steward left him in do doubt that were he to do so, such an application would also prove fruitless.

The Palace bell rang to signify the end of the day's classes, and Amrach suggested to his men, as he rejoined them, that if they were to get anything to eat then they should make their way as hastily as possible to the Refreshment House. However, on arriving they found it already full, so he decided that his men should return and join the rest of the company outside the village.

Strolling through the streets of Madon he came across the two men that he had met at the Refreshment House on the occasion of his first visit there.

'How do you fare, Sir?' one of them greeted him warmly. 'Is all well with you?'

'I am very well, thank you,' replied Amrach. 'And I am most grateful to you both for making it possible for me to get an audience with the Conclave. Had it not been for that introduction I would not have had the opportunity to address the residents of the Palace of Learning.'

Both men smiled and nodded their heads to show their acceptance of Amrach's expression of appreciation. Amrach noticed that though on their first meeting each wore two feathers in their lapels, one of yellow and one of red, today one of them had the yellow feather missing.

Aware that he was staring, Amrach, somewhat embarrassed, asked, 'Are you gentlemen off to the Refreshment House? For if you are, I am sorry to say that you will find it packed to the doors.'

'That was indeed our destination,' said the man with the two feathers. 'As it is, we will take a drink in our own rooms. You are very welcome, Sir, to join us if you have a mind to.'

Amrach thanked them for the invitation and said that he would be very pleased to accept. Before long, all three of them were seated in a comfortable suite which bore all the hallmarks of its owner's occupation.

Along one side of the room, bookshelves supported leather-bound volumes from floor to ceiling. Against another wall was a mahogany desk upon which stood pots of ink, documents and quills.

'A great deal has occurred since your last visit to us,' said the man with two feathers.

'Is that so?' replied Amrach.

'Does this mean that you are totally unaware of what has taken place in your absence?' said the man with the feather who looked at the other with uncertainty and not a little hesitation.

'I am aware of nothing,' said Amrach. 'You are the first people that I have had any conversation with, apart from a very brief encounter I had with the steward at the Palace of Learning.'

'I think you have seen the last of the interior of the oak chambers,' said the man who Amrach would later come to know as Entimos, and on whose lapel was only one red feather. 'The great reception that you received from the residents was not entirely welcomed by the Conclave.'

'So much so,' enjoined the man with two feathers, 'that a decree was passed that anyone who was found to be embracing the views that you espoused would be expelled from the Palace of Learning immediately, and without recourse to appeal. Not all the Conclave had been in agreement with this edict, but the ones who held the power prevailed.'

'In reality,' said Entimos, 'it was not what you said that caused such great offence, it was that you had taken away the focus from the roast duck issue. This was evidenced by the fact that it took the Palace cleaners a great deal of time to remove the hundreds of white and green feathers that had been strewn around the hall.'

At this the three of them laughed and laughed, unable to contain themselves at how ridiculous the situation had become.

'It would be laughable were it not also very sad,' said the man with two feathers. 'Around three hundred students have been expelled and, what is more, each member of the faculty has been asked to swear that they will not encourage any of the residents to join forces with you. If any of them refuse they have been advised that they will be disciplined and, if they continue with such attitudes, they too will be expelled and their careers brought to an end. You will probably have noticed that my colleague Entimos no longer carries the yellow feather which allows him to teach on The Current Edicts of the Lion. This is because he made it known that he would not denounce your words before the residents of the Palace.'

'Bless you!' said Amrach to Entimos. 'The Lion will surely reward you for your loyalty.'

'The real problem is the one posed by the man Qatsir,' Entimos said.

'Qatsir? I seem to know the name but—'

'You should remember him,' said Entimos, 'for was he not the man to whom you gave the authority to organize those who wished to join the Lion's army?'

'Yes, of course – that is where I heard the name. A man approached me shortly after I had addressed the residents and suggested that he consolidate the support, given the fact that I had said that I would be away for a time. Though then I did not know how long a time that would be.'

'He did that, all right,' said the man with two feathers, 'but on his own behalf rather than on yours.'

'What do you mean by that?'

'Well, as soon as you left, and while the residents were in great heart, he called a public meeting of his own. He told them that he spoke in your name and with your authority and so, understandably, was given the acclaim that you had received. They all listened in rapt attention. The platform that you gave him became a power base that he has used to his own advantage. I was present at the meeting and to begin with he spoke loyally of you.'

'What do you mean, "to begin with?"' asked Amrach, puzzled.

'Simply this,' said Entimos, 'that a few days later he called a second meeting, and this time his attitude changed. Having initially gained their ear by using you as an introduction, he now began to speak against you. Obliquely at first, but no one could be in any doubt what he was saying.'

'He asked what kind of leader would inspire and then just ride away. He queried the wisdom of being administered by someone sent from the Stronghold, such a great distance away. Would it not be better to submit their allegiance to someone nearer at hand? At the third meeting—'

'There was a third meeting?' enquired Amrach.

'There was a third and more besides,' said Entimos. 'You have heard nothing yet. At that meeting someone he had designated to introduce him did so with a clarion of trumpets calling out that all should stand before "the Great Warrior Qatsir".'

'I don't believe it!' laughed Amrach in astonishment.

'Believe it or not, it is true,' insisted Entimos. 'He then announced that "his" army was the only true army. He agreed that the Princes of Harag should be defeated but that this could only be done effectively under his leadership and his leadership alone. He then went on to say that the Paraclete had told him as much. This greatly impressed the residents as you might imagine. He demanded a high degree of personal submission to himself and his vision and made it clear that to disobey him was tantamount to rebelling against the Lion.

'Someone in the crowd called out, "But what if Amrach should return?" Qatsir responded by saying that if he did return he was very welcome to join him and fight by his side: as long as Amrach was willing to recognise the Great Warrior Qatsir as the true leader.'

'He actually referred to himself as the Great Warrior Qatsir?' asked Amrach.

'Most certainly,' said the man with two feathers, 'and a great number of people believe what he is saying. You see, many of them have only known the cold teaching of the Palace of Learning. They were greatly inspired by what you had to say but, when you left, Qatsir took advantage of the situation. It may be that his primary motive is power and prestige but the fact remains, he was here and you were not.'

'That is only because I was acting on orders from the Lion via the Paraclete.'

'Certainly,' said Entimos. 'But as my colleague has said, the situation has moved on at speed. It was as if you were used, by your powerful message, to break a dam of water that had been held up for generations. But now Qatsir has irrigated the streams in his direction, and for his own ends. Some are referring to those who have bonded themselves to him as the "Cult of Qatsir".'

Amrach protested that such an accusation may be unfair to Qatsir. However, the man with two feathers argued that it was not at all an unfair designation. He argued on the basis that any culture that was led by an inordinately dominant leader was in danger of becoming a cult.

'I assume,' said Entimos, 'that you are going challenge him over this?'

'Not at all,' said Amrach. 'I have acted in integrity in this matter. The only fault that can be laid against me is that, without consulting the Paraclete and because I thought no harm could be done, I allowed the man Qatsir to operate on my behalf. Yes, I did create a platform for him, but that is done now and cannot be undone.'

'But he has undermined you! It is surely essential that you retaliate, and with speed. How can you appear to be so detached from what amounts to a rebellion?'

'I am called to fight the Princes of Harag and no one else. As I have said, I have acted justly. It could be that he has a heart to fight the Princes of Harag, as I have. Perhaps his enthusiasm has got the better of him. The judgement of his motives rests with the Lion, not with me.'

'I can think of other motives for his actions,' suggested Entimos.

'And so can I,' said Amrach, 'but that is not the point. We must leave the matter with the Lion. If the man Qatsir has acted wrongly towards me, the Council of Theotes will deal with it. If he and his followers have lacked integrity then they will have built termites into the foundations of their purpose. They may not fall today and they may not fall tomorrow, but they will surely fall.

'There is however a matter, Entimos, that I would like you to attend to. I have to tell you, that should you wish to proceed with it, it may set you further at variance with the Conclave. Whether or not you decide to assist me with this is something that you must decide for yourself.'

'Speak on,' said Entimos.

'I will shortly be returning to my men. When I have gone I should like you to contact, as soon as you can, as many as possible of the residents that were expelled. Let them know that I have returned, as promised, and that we are stationed just outside the village limits. I shall wait there until this time tomorrow. But if that deadline is not met, I shall travel on. Are you willing?'

Before Entimos could answer, the man with two feathers interrupted.

'Amrach, with your permission, I should like to take on this responsibility myself.'

'You!' said Amrach. 'But to this point you have not been exposed to criticism from the Conclave.'

'Precisely so, but my position should have been compromised before now if I had been as sincere as Entimos. The time to take my stand is long overdue. In any event, my possession of two feathers gives me twice as much opportunity to make contact than is afforded to him.'

'Be it as you wish, my friend. As it is I must leave now. Thank you both for your hospitality. You have become companions in arms whether you wield a weapon or not. We have a great battle ahead and I am confident that the victory will be ours. Farewell!'

And with that, Amrach left the room and rejoined his men.

At the same time on the following day, many of the residents came over to his camp. It was clear, however, that the majority of the scholars had opted to follow Qatsir. Among those that joined Amrach were Entimos and his colleague. And now neither of them possessed feathers, of any hue, upon their person.

'I always thought of your friend as "the man with two feathers", but now I can no longer refer to him as that,' smiled Amrach.

'His name is Kalon,' advised Entimos.

13

The Return to the Stronghold

When Amrach arrived at the entrance to the Valley of Chanuts, and was faced once more with the two access roads, he made very sure this time to consult with the Paraclete.

'As you will remember,' the Paraclete said, 'one road is rough and the other smooth. The road you are to take is the smooth road.'

'Surely not – how can that be?' protested Amrach. 'On the last occasion I travelled this way I chose the smooth road and got into trouble for doing so!'

'You fell among thieves because you did not feel it necessary to consult the will of the Lion. The issue is not whether the road is rough or smooth, what matters is that you are careful to travel the road that the Lion considers best for you. When you were last here, the rough road would have been the better way. Today it is the smooth road that he wishes you to follow.'

'And are we to travel directly to Chaneph once we have passed through the valley?'

'That is indeed the path that you should tread.'

It was a pleasant journey that day as the long column travelled on. When they came to the part of the road that passed the inn where he had been robbed, Amrach imagined for a moment the look on the landlord's face, if he had dropped by with this great retinue. He was tempted, but resisted the inclination to find out.

The memories that he had of Chaneph were by no means sweet. All he wanted to do was to contact the dozen people who had pledged themselves to the cause, and travel onwards, as quickly as possible, to the Stronghold. However, that was not to be.

Before Amrach's army came in sight of the town, the serpentine line of soldiers had first to follow a winding lane that meandered on the perimeter of a small copse of trees. As Amrach and those who were nearest to him drew adjacent to the wooded area, a short fat man with squint eyes jumped out and into the path before them.

'Hello chummy, it's great to have you back!' the human roadblock said.

Amrach brought Morning Breeze to a sharp stop, dismounted and, flinging his arms around his friend cried out, 'Tumbleweed, you old rascal, how are you?'

'I am very well,' came back Tumbleweed's reply. 'It is the greatest of joys to see you chummy. You have been greatly missed – and what a great crowd follows in your wake!'

'It is great to see you too, but I hope your joy is not the result of an over-indulgence in that dreadful Honeydew!' Amrach teased.

'I have little need for it these days, chummy,' said Tumbleweed good-humouredly. 'Might I have the pleasure of accompanying you into the town? We have a surprise in store for you.'

Amrach was not too sure that he was ready for any more surprises. The revelation that had been sprung on him at Madon would keep him going for some time yet, he thought to himself. Yet there was no reason in the world that he should deny Tumbleweed his request. In any event, were he to bring his whole army into the town it may well be a reason for disquiet were the population of Chaneph to witness so many people travelling in one body.

Amrach asked his followers to move off the road and into the fields in order to take some rest. He informed them that he would be back presently, then he and Tumbleweed rode side by side into the town as they had done on a previous occasion, though in far different circumstances.

'How did you know when to expect me?' asked Amrach. 'You were clearly laying in wait for me as I passed by in order to ambush me, you rogue.'

'Oh, the Paraclete informed me,' retorted Tumbleweed nonchalantly.

'Did he indeed?' said Amrach, forgetting in that brief moment an important principle. It was not just leaders of armies, men like Zohah and prophetesses that could commune with the Paraclete. Tumbleweed and all who sought to follow the Lion had equal access to him.

'And what else did the Paraclete tell you, may I ask?' enquired Amrach.

'Only how many would be travelling with you, and perhaps a few other things besides,' said Tumbleweed as he brought his old horse to a standstill.

'Now look across there,' he motioned to Amrach.

He was gesturing to a large grassy amphitheatre, the one that had been the scene of so much disappointment to Amrach in the not-too-distant past. Again, it was totally packed with people.

'Not another festival, I hope, Tumbleweed?' said Amrach, trying to disguise his feelings.

'Not quite, chummy. These people are the rest of your army!'

'My what?' exclaimed Amrach, his mouth open and his eyes agog.

'Yes, your army,' came the confirmatory reply.

'But there are more over there than I have with me now, and I left so few of you behind!'

'About a dozen,' said Tumbleweed.

'Then how . . . ?' Now it was Amrach's turn to gesture towards the grassy slopes.

'There was much searching of heart after you had gone. Many found it hard to sleep that night and, on the day following the Festival, people talked of little else. The result is what you see before you. It is the Blacksmith that you have to thank for bringing them together.'

'Ah, the Blacksmith,' said Amrach, as his mind's eye brought the man's muscular frame into sharper perspective. 'The one who considered himself of so little value to the Lion's cause.'

'Hello chummy, are you still there?' asked Tumbleweed mischievously, in an attempt to bring back Amrach from what he thought was a daydream.

'I'm sorry, Tumbleweed. It's just that . . . Well, I'm amazed!'

'Let's go across and meet them. You will of course be willing to address them, I presume?'

Amrach walked along the long rocky plateau. There was no wooded dais there now as there had been at the Festival. There was no bunting and no torches but, as it was light, everyone could see him and he was sure that he would be able to make his voice heard.

He was welcomed with huge enthusiasm and there was no heckling on this occasion. The people hung on his every word. He told them about the many that had joined him and who were, at this very moment, outside the town.

When he had fully finished speaking a robed figure approached him from the side of the crowd. He recognised the form as that of the Seer who had interrupted what he had said when last he had stood upon this very spot. As the Seer came closer he raised his hand in a way that signified to Amrach that he had not come to contradict him today.

'If I might speak to them?'

Amrach nodded in consent.

'The past few days have given me much time to think and not a little reason to feel ashamed. We did not treat Amrach well on the last occasion he was with us. Yet, although he had departed, the power of his words remained behind to challenge us. While he was here, he watched as we held a great feast in honour of days gone by. Tonight we will eat a great feast in honour of days that are to come. The day of the Lion's victory over the Princes of Harag!'

As the Seer was speaking, thunderous applause rang out from every corner and resounded around the town.

Amrach's eyes were wet with tears. Not in sadness as before, but in worship of the Mighty Three that he should ever have the privilege of witnessing such a day.

Tumbleweed was commissioned to go out to the troops and bring them into the town that they might be given the very best of hospitality for the night.

Amrach sought out the Blacksmith and both rejoiced together. What a changed man! His head was held high, not in arrogance and presumption, but like a man consumed with purpose and a sense of destiny. His eyes were as bright as his confidence was strong: not in himself but in the power of the Lion and of the certainty of victory.

'I suppose our friend Tumbleweed has given you the details of the remarkable occurrences over the past few days,' said the Blacksmith to Amrach as they embraced.

'Only briefly. He said that the people had found it difficult to sleep that night, and made their way in groups from all over the town back to the amphitheatre. What happened then?'

'It was truly amazing,' said the Blacksmith. 'Nobody co-ordinated this, you must understand; it is as if every home had received its own message to go back out into the night. If you had been standing on the rocky plateau and looking down at the town you would have seen the lights in windows as candles were lit in home after home. The streets were filled at dead of night as if it were the middle of the day. Those who did not get to the amphitheatre because of their anguish sat at the side of the roads with their friends. Some were weeping, many were sobbing profusely.

'The twelve of us who had committed to your message were already by the grassy slopes. We had not even attempted to go home. We could never have slept in a thousand years. The challenge was still burning in our hearts and all we wanted to do was to talk to one another about its implications. Not that we were afraid – it was just that we were so excited and so amazed that the Lion would consider including the likes of us in his purposes.

'There was a slight element of confusion,' admitted the Blacksmith as he went on. 'I think that it was Tumbleweed in our small group that brought it to the surface. You see, we started to think about you. It was all well and good us watching this transformation before our eyes and seeing an entire town being changed in a night. We were thinking about how you must be feeling. We imagined you travelling onwards with a heavy heart. The last remembrance we had of you were your tears and disappointment and then, of course, had no idea how long or short a time it would be until you came back.'

'Well, you were certainly right about my sentiments,' said Amrach. 'I felt not only that I had been rejected by the town – that was bad enough – but worse still, I felt that I had failed the Lion.'

'However, what a sight it must have been for you!' said Amrach in an attempt to deflect the attention away from himself for a moment. 'I trust that thoughts of me did not leave your spirits too heavy, and spoil what must have been one of the most joyous moments of your life.'

'Our hearts were burdened, it was true – but then something very strange began to happen.'

'Within the amphitheatre?' asked Amrach.

'No – among our tiny group,' the Blacksmith said. 'We all began to shake. We were terrified at first, not knowing what would happen – but then we heard a voice. It was the Paraclete. We knew he spoke to you; and might even speak to you about us, but we never dreamed that he would make himself known to us personally.

'He explained many things. We spoke with him, and he with us, for a long time. I do not know how long it was, but we noticed that the sun was beginning to rise and that a new day was about to dawn. He put us at rest too with regard to our concern about you. He comforted us by saying – what a comforter he is, Amrach – he comforted us by saying that his words, like seeds, sometimes take a time to grow. He told how the words that you had planted were being fruitful within hours. There were times, he said, when it took years – but every seed that was sown would bring a harvest one day. Isn't that wonderful, Amrach?'

'Yes,' said Amrach, 'it is indeed truly wonderful.'

The two major strands of the armies converged and made great progress though the whole of the following day.

Negotiating the woods took time and effort but the people were in such great heart that the time passed quickly enough. There was no question of stopping by Berekah's cottage, but Amrach would have loved to do so if only for Berekah to see the result of his sowing of both hospitality and a leather bag of coins. 'How many links there are,' thought Amrach, 'in the chain of the Lion's purpose!'

However, Amrach need not have worried. Berekah had been informed by the Paraclete of the armies' progress and was out to meet them.

'Greetings to you, good Berekah!' called Amrach from the road. 'Yet another item for your treasure house of stories with which you can entertain those to whom you give the freedom of your home.'

'Blessings upon your head, faithful Amrach,' the old man called back. 'I in my old age, pray that the Mighty Three will continue to guide and guard your every step.'

When Amrach had first come upon the Stronghold, it had been by the light of day. By the time that the army had emerged from the forest, night had fallen – and what a sight filled their vision!

Although no torches gave their glow or fires lit the night, the whole area was bathed in light. For a second time Amrach witnessed the effulgence that emanated from the castle walls. He glanced back to ensure that all his men were safely out of the wood. There was total silence. No one stirred. The shafts of light that streamed from the castle illuminated every face. For most it was their first encounter, yet all were affected by the awesome sight. It was a picture unparalleled.

It was not until Amrach actually called them forward that anyone dared make a move but, at his command, the stream of valiant folk moved on.

As they came to the approach road, one of the riders struck up the Lion's song that Amrach had first heard at

Chaneph. On the first occasion he had heard it it had filled him with joy, and on the next occasion with a deep sadness. This night, as again he heard the words, he was filled with a sense of overwhelming wonder. As each of those who rode took up the words there rose a great, majestic, mobile anthem:

> Hail to the Lion, Mighty King
> And Victor over all his foes!
> From sea to sea his people come
> To give him praise and to adore.
> What tongue can tell or lips recite
> The Greatness of his name?
> From coast to coast the nations tell
> His splendour and his fame!

They sang it over and over again until the head of the column, lead by Amrach, was within sight of the gates of the Stronghold. Then, for a reason no one there could comprehend, they all paused. At that precise moment, from the turrets and towers of the castle walls, came a sound like a million trumpets in magnificent fanfare. Then, as the fortress gates swung slowly open, from the terraces, from the courtyard, from every parapet and tower, rang the myriad voices of assembled choirs and, together in orchestrated depth, all sang out the anthem yet again.

Riders dismounted from their horses and joined those on foot, who now lay prostrate on the ground unable to contain sight or sound of what was taking place before them. When courage bade them raise their eyes, they saw amid the Stronghold's massive gates, clothed in splendour, none other than the Lion himself.

'Come forward, Amrach,' the Lion summoned.

Amrach rose slowly to his feet and began to make his way towards him.

'I introduce you to your army, Sire,' began Amrach. 'These faithful people have pledged themselves to be your loyal subjects, and have devoted themselves to fight against the Princes of Harag. They wait only for your command.'

'You have done well, Amrach, very well – and you have proved yourself worthy of the Sceptre you were given. The Paraclete has told me much about your exploits and commends you for your courage. Doubtless you have learned many lessons on the way, and feel a good deal stronger now than on the day you first set out.'

'Indeed, your Majesty, instruction has been gleaned as much by my failures as through any successes I may have had.'

'I am glad to hear you say that,' said the Lion. 'It reveals to me that you are continuing to grow. Of course you are not yet released from the task before you, and you will need to continue to build strength upon strength. My watchmen have brought me intelligence of the latest movements of the Princes of Harag. They have fully consolidated their position within the land from which you originally came. They are now already a day's journey from the Plains of Shephelah.'

'When then may we march against them?' asked Amrach urgently.

'You, together with others of my Commanders, will set out to meet them on the day after tomorrow. Until then, shelter, food and everything you need will be made available for those who have travelled with you. After you have rested for the night you will be invited to the Great Hall where an important meeting will take place around dawn. Is all this clear to you?'

'Yes, Sire,' said Amrach reverently and knew, for that moment at least, that his audience with the Lion had come to a close.

14

The Day of Preparation

The next morning Amrach was woken early by a knock at the door of his bed chamber. It was none other than Aspasmos who had come personally to welcome him to the Stronghold and to announce the time of the Lion's court.

All who were in attendance heard the Lion speak of plans that he and his Commanders had made for the rest of the day, for on the morrow they would march to the Plains.

The Commanders addressed the many that had come with Amrach. For the first time they were referred to as The Lion's Army. Amrach looked across the gathered throng as he listened intently to the instructions that they were being given. He gazed with gratitude over those who had come from different towns and backgrounds but who were now united in a common vision.

'And so to the matter of armour . . .' Amrach heard one of the Commanders say as his mind was brought rapidly back from the past to the present. He watched an attendant as he displayed each item and as its purpose and importance were explained.

There were two aspects of the armour that had to be remembered at all costs. The first was that if one part of the armour was missing, the warrior would be rendered as vulnerable as if he were wearing no part of the armour at all. The second principle was that there was no covering for the back as it was assumed that the wearer would never be in retreat.

This explained, the Commander pointed out the various features of the helmet, breastplate, shield, belt and shoes.

'I would now like to draw your attention to the sword,' he continued. 'Its design is such that its skilful use will be an advantage both in defence and attack. Ensure that you keep it with you at all times, however fierce the battle. Though your enemy is vastly more experienced than many of you, none of them has at their disposal weapons such as yours. The power of this sword lies not in the dexterity of the user, but principally in the strength of the weapon itself.'

'Remember my words carefully,' he stated with emphasis, 'Stand your ground and you will be a victor: turn your back and you become a victim. This will be our watchword.'

The men and women – for there were many women in the Lion's army – noted the words well and spontaneously repeated the phrase out loud in order to give it force. The very walls of the Stronghold echoed with the sound of it. The hearing of the statement spoken by so many, thought Amrach, strengthened their resolve and encouraged their hearts as much as the stating of the words themselves.

Only the Commanders knew how important that truth would prove to be within the next few days.

The following morning before sunrise Amrach was summoned for an audience with the Lion. Only his immediate Commanders were with him in the Great Hall. There were no choirs, musicians or audience on this occasion. Not even the Daughters of Zohah were there.

'Amrach, come forward and stand before me,' the Lion began. 'This day is the day on which the battle will be joined. It is for this moment that you first crossed the Plains of Shephelah and made your journey towards the land of Phos. Tell me, what are your feelings at such a time as this?'

'I feel anxious, Sire. Not for my safety, for I feel secure within the Lion's care. I am anxious to begin, to commence, to engage the forces of Harag in battle.'

'I am sure that you are, Amrach, and you shall have your wish in not many hours time. What do you know of the Princes of Harag?'

'Very little of their origins, your Majesty,' replied Amrach. 'I know only of the devastation and horror that follows in their wake. I know first hand of the pain and suffering that they bring. I know that they are cruel taskmasters to those who are their slaves and that their dominion is one of darkness and destruction. Yet these facts alone are more than enough to compel me to play my part in rising against them and seeking to emancipate those that they hold in their iron grip.'

'Then it seems you are not aware that they once were in my service and numbered among my own Commanders?'

'I am not, Sire; how could such a thing be?'

'A long time ago, when the Council of Theotes first appointed those who would serve us with authority and responsibility, there was a great Prince among them that you now know to be Harag. He was of great importance in the Stronghold, so much so that, outside the Mighty Three, he was the most powerful of all. As time went by he expressed a desire to be equal with the Council of Theotes and, when this was refused, stirred up a rebellion.'

'A rebellion here, Sire – in the Stronghold of Theotes itself?'

'In this very place,' confirmed the Lion. 'The Prince stirred up dissention among many of our people and, as soon as the rebellion was brought to our knowledge, it was dealt with forcefully. The Prince, and all those who were deceived into following him, were thrown out of the Stronghold. They have never been back within its walls to this day – although we know of course that their emissaries have travelled the length and breadth of the land of Phos with a view to undermining the authority of this kingdom.'

'Then this is the rebellion that is mentioned in the Remnant Legend and of which no account has been retained,' said Amrach.

'That is so. The Princes of Harag were successful in keeping this from the population of your land, but underestimated the courage of those who would make it their purpose to hold on to the truths contained in fragments of parchments that remained.'

'Your Majesty, may I venture to ask you a question?' said Amrach with a measure of timidity.

'Ask on.'

'As you are all powerful, why did you allow the Prince the power to make a choice to rebel against you? A great deal of suffering would have been spared, would it not, your majesty?'

Amrach could hardly believe that he was questioning the Lion. Yet he sensed no anger towards him. On the contrary he felt a sense of acceptance of him that clothed him like a blanket. He was being given permission to be real. He was being allowed to be himself.

'I can understand you thinking that,' the Lion responded. 'You are not the first mortal to raise such a question. You are wise when you speak to me of "choice". Cast your mind back to when your children were small. What was it that gave you the most joy?'

'There were so many things . . .' began Amrach, a lump coming to his throat, 'but I suppose it was when they ran and threw their arms around me—'

'Because you "made them do it," I suppose' said the Lion.

'Of course not, your Majesty, they did it because they wanted to. It would have meant nothing if they had been forced.'

'Then,' said the Lion, 'you will understand how love is expressed out of choice – even though it brings a shadow side.'

'I don't understand . . .'

'Well,' continued the Lion, 'surely you see that when a created being has the choice to love it also has the choice not to love. The shadow side is rebellion.'

'I think I am beginning to understand,' Amrach responded. 'But may I be permitted, Sire, to ask one further question?'

'Speak on.'

'Why, when the rebellion took place, did you not destroy the Prince and those that followed him?'

'The choice between love and rebellion', the Lion went on, 'is the test by which all created beings are judged. There is no other way of knowing what lies within the heart. Words can have many meanings, but love and rebellion lie at the heart of every decision in the universe.'

It was then that Amrach remembered what Zohah had once told him, 'A day will come when all must sit down to a Banquet of Consequences.'

The Lion read his thoughts and continued:

'Amrach, let me tell you something. There is not one soul that I have ever brought into being that I have ever annihilated – brought to the end of its consciousness. I do not speak of rocks and trees and physical objects, I speak of the souls of men, women and Commanders – beings that can come under judgement.

'The Mighty Three have existed eternally, but that is not true for you and those that you know. There was a time when you were not. When I created the universe you were not. When the walls of this Stronghold were built you were not. Even Zohah and Berekah were given breath before you entered your mother's womb.

'Now listen carefully to my words,' the Lion continued. 'Once given life, there will never be a time when you will cease to be. Mortal men whose bodies die never cease to be. They live on. My Commanders will live on for ever in my presence and the Princes of Harag will live on for ever under my judgement. You can be sure Amrach, all will live on.

'Think of this, Amrach, as you enter battle this day: although unlike the Council of Theotes you had a beginning, because you follow closely in our path, like us you will never cease to be.'

Amrach had learned many things during his conversations with the Paraclete, but this teaching from the Lion surpassed all the revelation he had ever heard. Could this really be true? It must be, for he had heard it with his own ears and from none other than the Lion himself.

'But now,' said the Lion, 'I must tell you of the order of battle and how you shall ride out from this place. All my Commanders have agreed . . .'

As he said this, the Lion moved his head from side to side and, as his gaze made contact with his mighty men, they all nodded their assent and signalled their agreement.

'All of my Commanders have agreed that you, Amrach, should ride alongside the chief of all my Commanders on this day of days.'

'No, Sire – that can never be!' Amrach interrupted. 'I have no experience in battle. I am less knowledgeable in matters of war than any in this Great Hall. I was commissioned only to raise the army and, though I will fight to the end of my strength if needs be, I have no desire to ride in such a place of high honour.'

'Silence, Amrach!' the Lion said sternly. 'You cannot say "No" and "Sire" within the same breath. It is a contradiction. Which of the words will you say? The choice is yours!'

Amrach paused for a moment, greatly taken aback. It had needed great courage in the first place to seek an audience with the Lion. He had never thought for one moment that he would then be the recipient of the Silver Sceptre and be commissioned to go on so great an assignment. It was one thing, however, to lead an army to the Stronghold. It was quite another leading them next to his Chief Commander and into battle. What could he do? How would he respond? If he said 'No' he could not then say 'Sire'; and if he said 'Sire', he could not say 'No'.

'I will call you "Sire". I will continue in obedience. Forgive me I—'

'That is good,' interjected the Lion. 'Now I will introduce you to the Commander with whom you shall ride and lead my troops into battle.'

Amrach looked to the left and right of the throne as the Lion motioned him to come forward but no one stirred. He then heard the tall doors of the Great Hall behind him begin to swing open. He turned to look and saw . . . Darak!

'Yes,' said the Lion, 'it is indeed Darak with whom you will ride. He is the bravest and noblest of my men. He is my Chief Commander.'

The two embraced warmly as they met but, realising before whom they stood and knowing that he had much to say, they stood together side by side in silence in order that he might continue.

'The cries of the sufferers scourged by the Princes of Harag has come often to our ears, but it was not then the time to act. When the right season was upon us, their forces invaded your land. You may have thought, Amrach, that it was you that decided to cross the Plains of Shephelah to come for help. It was not so. Though you knew it not, it was the Paraclete that put it within your heart. He was out seeking after you long before you sought to hear his voice or even knew of his existence. My watchmen observed you, and covered you, from the moment you began your journey. When your mount stumbled and you were thrown to the ground – even then you were within their sight. It was Darak that was sent out to rescue you. You were chosen for this mission. It was never necessary that you were gifted or even that you were strong. It was only necessary that you were willing.'

'I am speechless,' confessed Amrach.

'There is nothing more to say,' replied the Lion. 'But before you leave, take these.'

Two stewards came forward carrying a cushion and gave to Amrach and to Darak – a Silver Sceptre.

15

The Battle of Shephelah

Amrach and Darak left the Great Hall together. The sun had risen and, as they entered the courtyard, they were greeted by the sound of much activity and an atmosphere of anticipation.

'The first thing that we must do is to collect your suit of armour,' Darak suggested as he guided Amrach through the bustling throng.

On reaching the armoury, Amrach was supplied with a suit identical to the one that Darak wore. The helmet was the same, as were the breastplate, the belt, the shield and the shoes.

When Amrach commented on the match, Darak smiled and motioned towards the people who had already received their supplies. Not only were they also dressed identically, but so also would be every warrior in the Lion's army. Amrach's surprise was so evident that Darak explained.

'Do you see that foot soldier over there?' he said pointing. 'His helmet is made of the finest material that the land of Phos can produce. Nothing in the entire universe can equal its design. The same rule applies to every aspect of his armour. To be secure in battle one must be willing to wear it in the prescribed way and remember never to turn one's back on the enemy. In other words, its protection cannot be improved upon and, as we are wearing it, neither can ours.'

'And now, Amrach, take up your sword,' continued Darak as the steward passed it across to him. 'This too is the same in strength and quality as all that will be wielded today.'

Amrach wrapped his hand around the hilt as the weapon was offered to him.

'It's just perfect. It feels as if it had been made just for me,' he said as he caressed its contours admiringly. 'The balance is right, as is the weight. It's absolutely perfect.'

'It's a remarkable weapon in many ways. Although every man and women in the Lion's army is different, even so, every one of them will echo the very same words that you have said when they first handle it. That is because each of them personally, as individuals, has chosen to enlist in the Lion's army. If one of our enemies were to take hold of this weapon it would be unwieldy in their hands. The weapon can never be used effectively against us. There have been times when those that work against us have tried to imitate and to copy, but they have never succeeded. This is not to say that they do not have powerful weapons of their own. They do, and we would be very wrong indeed to underestimate them.'

As Darak concluded his description of the sword, the trumpeters that stood on the walls of the fortress sounded out a loud blast upon their golden instruments.

'That is the signal for all the troops to gather,' said Darak. 'It is time for us to find our horses, for in a few moments we will be called upon to lead our people out. The responsibility of the other Commanders is to marshal the Lion's army in ordered ranks. When that has been done a signal will be sent to us, and we will set out from the Stronghold, along the approach road and then left toward the Plains.'

Moments later a second blast of trumpets rang out over the towers of the Stronghold and the two friends pulled their horses into a steady canter and rode out together at the head of the column. After a little while, and at a signal from Darak, they turned their mounts round to face those that followed them. Darak projected his voice so as many as possible could hear what he said:

'Fellow warriors, this is a great day for us all. We have been informed by our Watchmen that our enemies, the Princes of Harag, are even now upon the Plains. Yet we are more than a match for them as we go forth in the Lion's name. Be strong. Be steadfast. Be courageous and, what ever you face this day, settle it well in your mind that you will stand firm. Remember, "Stand your ground and you are a victor – turn your back and you are a victim." So then what is it that we will be today as we ride forth?'

'Victors in the Lion's name!' the people chanted over and over again.

'On then!' commanded Darak. 'To the Plains!'

When they left the approach road and came to the brow of the hill, and were about to set out to the west, Amrach noticed something strange coming from an eastward direction in a great cloud of dust. He pointed it out to Darak who, on seeing it and hearing the thunderous noise that accompanied it, called the army to a halt.

As it came nearer they noticed several hundred riders approaching at great speed. They knew it could not be the bloodline of Harag for their enemy would only be one third of the way across the Plains and that in an opposite direction. Who then could it be?

The riders came to a standstill some distance away and, as they did, one man left the group and rode towards them.

'I greet you, Amrach.'

'I greet you too Sir, and, if you will remove your helmet, I will also have the advantage of knowing to whom I am speaking.'

The man did so and was immediately recognised by Amrach as Qatsir.

Amrach turned to Darak, as if by way of explanation and in order to introduce the stranger, but before he could do so Qatsir cut in on him and said:

'No Sir, with respect, I feel it is my responsibility to explain to the Commander and not yours. My name is Qatsir and I come from Madon. When Amrach came to speak to our people of the raising of an army, I used the incident to draw people to myself. In doing so I caused split and division by my action. When Amrach left, I too experienced dissention within my own ranks and believe it to be a result of my own attitude. I have reaped only what I have sown. I have been humbled by the snare of my pride and desire for self-advancement, and come to you Amrach to publicly ask for your forgiveness.'

Amrach was anxious to advance towards the battle lines but sensed that the man before him was sincere in his repentance so, addressing him, said, 'I believe, Qatsir, that you are sincere in what you say and, as far as I am concerned the past should remain where it belongs – behind us.'

'Then may I and my men ride with you into battle?'

'That is something that you must ask the Commander.'

'I have no problem with that,' said Darak, 'if that is what you wish. You must however first ride to the

Stronghold and make sure that your people are fully equipped for battle before you leave.'

Amrach wondered, as Qatsir and those that followed him rode in the opposite direction towards the Stronghold, if they would be recognised by Entimos and Kalon as they travelled past the ranks. If so, he hoped that their hearts would be encouraged and not hurt. It was surely right that warriors of a like mind should ride together in unity.

As they approached the edge of the Plains the terrain became noticeably more difficult. Amrach looked round at the soldiers that followed. What a glorious sight they were! Outwardly their bright armour glistened and the faces that he was able to pick out reflected the fact that inwardly they were similarly ready and prepared for war.

They travelled a great distance across Shephelah, and then Darak and Amrach were brought to a standstill by the quiet voice of the Paraclete.

'They are not far ahead,' he whispered. 'In a short time now you will sense their presence and they yours. Be valiant. Remember, the armour that you wear is sufficient for you. Call your men to hold their swords before them when the bloodline of Harag advances upon them!'

Hardly had the Paraclete finished speaking when dreadful screams rent the air. It was the mingled sound of anger, violence, hate and terror. It was evident that the Princes of Harag had sensed that the Lion's army was in their path.

Turning to his men, Darak called out:

'Do not be afraid of their cries. It is not their screams that can harm you. Do not be terrified by terror or fearful of fear. Advance onwards towards them.'

The terrible shrieks intensified in volume and indicated that the enemy was nearing. The sky that had once been bright now turned black in the distance.

Clouds of dust billowed, beaten from the ground by the advancing horsemen as they pounded their way forward as if to the accompaniment of a million drums. Darak called to his Commanders to organise the warriors in wide ranks, and this they did.

'Stand firm!' he shouted, across the din of the approaching cavalry.

The Princes of Harag, each riding a jet black mount, looked like hideous giants on horseback as they raced in their hoards closer and closer still.

'Hold your ground!' roared Darak.

Their faces were grotesque beyond description. Their visages were contorted with rage. Their nostrils heaved with hateful vengeance. Their blood-red bulging eyes spat anger towards those who had dared to stand in their path.

They had thought that they had had their own way for centuries. They had believed that, having caused dissention in the Stronghold that all the Dominion would eventually be theirs. The exploits of these audacious sceptre-carriers had infuriated them. They were incensed at the accounts that they had heard of healing, health and emancipation among those that they had believed to be eternally held captive by their will.

'Swords forward!' Darak commanded.

They were very near now. Again Amrach glanced at the Lion's brave warriors. Each one stood tenaciously in their place. No one moved. Without exception they held their powerful swords obediently forward in front of them.

Amrach returned his focus to the oncoming hoards. The air was black with them. Their leader spurred his horse onward making directly for him and for Darak. This one was different from the rest. He was not grotesque or ugly – rather he was handsome with perfectly formed features – though it seemed that his blue eyes exuded more hate in them than all his evil forces put together.

Amrach and Darak increased their grip upon their swords. They were to take the first awful ferocity of the attack. The chief Prince of Harag fell upon them with a vengeful scream.

Amrach's heart beat faster. His lungs heaved heavily. His pulse raced. He thought of the Lion. He brought to mind the victims of the plague and the sight of the Children of Nasham. Then his thoughts flashed momentarily to the sight of his dead wife. This is why he was here. His muscles rippled and tensed. He stood firm as did Darak.

Across the battlefield the rest of the Lion's warriors were engaged. The sound of metal upon metal rent the air as shields and swords beat against one another. Seething rage poured from the throats of Harag's demonic battalions as they continued their assault and, as they cut and thrust, the Lion's army parried and took the battle to them.

The Chief Prince, the one who hated and despised the Lion the most, thrashed and lunged. Again the Lion's two most powerful warriors held their positions. How long the battle raged no one knew.

Simultaneously, holding their swords in their right hands, Amrach and Darak reached with their left hands into the leather coverings slung across their backs, and from the pouches revealed aloft the Silver Sceptres.

The Chief Prince wailed and writhed in recognition and foamed in rage before them. Then, his horse rearing up at the sight, threw its rider to the ground. He scrambled to his feet and, with fury firing his frenzy screamed at his devilish princes: 'Kill them, kill every one of them! Let none escape alive! Slay them all! Cut them down!'

Spontaneously, the warriors who had come from the Stronghold shouted, 'All hail the Lion! We stand victorious in his name! Secure are we in his armour! None can stand before his sword!'

Line after line of the bloodline of Harag fell upon the Lion's army but at every onslaught they were rendered powerless. Though they rained spears and darts of fire, the shields of the Lion's armoury proved sufficient.

Darak and Amrach dismounted and stood over the writhing form of the Chief Prince of Harag.

'We bind you in the Lion's name and, with the authority of his sceptre, we hold you and your hordes captive to his power.'

The chief Prince attempted to shield his face from the Sceptre; his wails now weakening to a whimper. Those who were still standing of his once-mighty warriors, fell to their knees – not in submission, but because they no had no power at all to stand. Amrach had not the least doubt that, were strength restored to them, they would rise up again with venom to fight. Their bearing emanated not from a surrender of their will but was the posture of whipped wolves.

Great cheers of rejoicing rose from the Lion's army. Darak had something to say to them, but allowed them their well-earned period of celebration. However, after some time had elapsed, he called them to give him their full attention.

'Look well upon these fallen hordes, and note this. Never again will the Princes of Harag bring oppression and cruelty upon our people. Never again will their emissaries spread lies, dissention and plague among our citizens. Today the slave-drivers are themselves enslaved, and the oppressors themselves are shackled. In the Lion's name, and by his great might, we have utterly destroyed the destroyer.'

The beaten Princes continued to writhe and snarl upon the ground, but could do nothing. They beat their gnarled fists but were helpless. The swords of the Lion and the declaration that his warriors had made over them had brought them to their knees, never again to rise.

Much cheering followed. So much in fact, that even Darak found it difficult to quell.

'But hear me on,' he continued, eventually prevailing upon the ecstatic assembly. 'This day will be inscribed eternally in the Book of Remembrance, and when it is written it shall be said that the Lion's sword secured the victory and his armour kept us safe. All hail the Mighty Three! All hail the Council of Theotes! All hail the Great Invisible One! All hail the Lion and the Paraclete who does their bidding!'

'All hail! All hail! All hail!' the people shouted as if their lungs would burst.

'Our mission is not yet ended as there is yet more to do,' Darak went on.

Amrach was puzzled. What more could there be to do? Surely this was the end of the matter. The Princes of Harag had been defeated and bound. What more could be asked for than that?

Darak turned to his friend as if reading his thoughts and, addressing him within the hearing of the army, said:

'Our forces will escort the beaten hordes of Harag back to the Stronghold of Theotes to await the final judgement of the Lion. The Great Invisible One has committed judgement into his hands. Amrach has yet to finally complete his mission.'

Amrach's face creased questioningly.

'He must go to announce to his own land the news of this great victory. Then he will return to us at the

Stronghold. He left that place in weakness, sorrowing and with a heavy heart. Now he must return a conqueror, a victor in the Lion's name.'

The two men embraced and parted. Darak led the army to the Stronghold and Amrach, travelling yet further west along the Plains, went on alone.

16

The Great Liberation

What Darak had said made great sense, thought Amrach. It would surely be wrong for him to return rejoicing to the Stronghold in the knowledge that there were those who needed to hear the message of the great victory on the Plains of Shephelah.

The trek over the vast wasteland was arduous, but the time seemed to pass much quicker than on his first attempt. His horse Morning Breeze had proved to be every bit as trustworthy as Berekah had promised. 'Sure of foot on stony ground and fleet of foot in battle' had been his words. How right they were. Amrach patted the long neck of his steed and his horse waved his head from side to side and snorted, as if in mutual appreciation.

He came upon his farm and found that it had been reduced to ruins and razed to the ground. The charred and toppled timbers lay as a sad monument to the destructive forces of Harag. At least, he thought, no one else would suffer as he had done, now that the evil Princes were bound and awaited the judgement that would come from the Lion's throne. He foraged among the rubble and the ashes for even the smallest memento of his former family, but found none.

The place was empty and still. Only in the corridors of memory could he hear the laughter of his wife and the banter of his sons.

'What am I to do next?' Amrach asked as he spoke with the Paraclete.

'You must travel on to the quarry,' the Paraclete replied.

'What quarry? There has been no quarrying here for many years.'

'When you left to ride across the Plains of Shephelah towards the Stronghold, the Princes of Harag took all the inhabitants of this area to an old disused quarry. Many died under their scourge, but there are still some who are alive. The quarry, and the mines that lead from it, are guarded by the servants of Harag. You will not find them an obstacle to you because, now the great battle is over, their strength is gone. The recent victory has removed from them the power that they once had. You must nevertheless watch out for the guards as you enter.'

When Amrach reached the perimeter of the quarry he noticed the guard's hut by an iron gate. Were it full he assumed it could contain around thirty to forty people. From where he stood he could see no activity in the area until, drawing nearer, he was able to pick out the silhouetted shapes of a few guards that lined what he was to discover was the main entrance to the mine.

Still wearing his armour and carrying his sword, he made his way stealthily to the hut, burst open the door and challenged the occupants.

'Stand back in the Lion's name!' he commanded as he advanced towards around thirty or so of the men who had been sitting at tables playing a game of dice.

They went for their weapons the moment he entered; dice and money cascaded to the floor in the confusion.

However, not one of them had the ability to draw their weapons. The sight of the Sceptre and the power of the sword were far too much for them.

'Who are you, and what is your business with us?' their leader snarled: his words and posture far more violent than his present strength could mirror.

'My name is Amrach and, although you do not know me, I come in the authority of one who is far greater than I and whose name may well be known to you – the Lion.'

The guards attempted a derisive laugh but, in their condition, it was as much as they could do to draw breath. Amrach continued:

'I am here to announce to you that all the Princes of Harag have been defeated at a great battle on the Plains of Shephelah by the Lion's forces.

'Not the Chief Prince as well? That cannot be!' one of them whimpered.

'The Chief Prince especially,' underlined Amrach forcefully. 'All of them of them have been led captive to the Stronghold of Theotes to await the Lion's will.'

'That cannot be!' another gasped. 'We were promised before they left that there would be hundreds more slaves for this very mine.'

'What you were promised I neither know or care. What I can assure you is that your leaders have suffered a defeat from which they will never recover. My purpose here is to free the slaves that you have held all this time in bondage.'

'You will not free them, for they are chained and we have the keys!' the leader snapped.

'You may growl all you wish, but you shall give me the keys at my bidding,' said Amrach, and seeing them around the leader's belt, reached for them and took them from him. The man tried, but was helpless to resist.

Amrach made his way to the mouth of the mine. At the sight of the Silver Sceptre the remaining guards that had not been in the hut, dropped to their knees.

The place was dark and damp and the stench dreadful. As Amrach approached, the sound of dragging chains became audible – and a vision of his terrifying dream of the Children of Nasham momentarily flashed before him.

What he was to discover here were not infants but adults, men and women, the elderly and those once youthful who had become haggard and worn by their enforced servitude. Their faces were blackened and their clothes ragged and filthy. They cowered as he came closer. Gently he told them that he had come to deliver them from the wretched place and informed them that they were now free people once again.

To his absolute amazement no one moved. He had fully anticipated that his words would be greeted with bursts of joy, but nothing could be further from the truth. He had not expected for a moment that his emancipating words would be met by silence.

'Did you not hear what I said?' Amrach repeated louder. 'The Princes of Harag are defeated and you are all free. Do you not understand? Free!'

Still no one moved, except in a few cases some skeletal forms cowered deeper into the darkness.

Amrach could see, even in this dim light, that each person's leg was circled by an iron shackle through which a long chain was looped which served to keep them all together. At one end of the chain was a heavy iron lock. He took the keys that he had taken from the guards and turned it. As he did so, one length of the chain fell to the ground. Slowly and carefully he pulled the length of cruel metal through each loop until everyone was free.

Still no one moved.

'I shall detach the irons from your legs once we get out into the fresh air and the sunlight,' said Amrach in the hope that this world provoke a response.

Still there was neither sound nor movement.

'Embrace them!' said the Paraclete.

'Embrace them?' echoed Amrach, 'What difference is that going to make? The stench in this place is almost unbearable as it is!'

'Embrace them,' said the Paraclete with a gentle firmness.

Obediently, Amrach went across to a man who stood at the beginning of the long line. The linking chain was now gone but they all remained in the same formation as if it was still present. Amrach, exactly as instructed by the Paraclete, extended his arms and held the man close.

Immediately, the man began to weep, and his entire frame began to be convulsed and to heave under the intensity of his sobs. As Amrach held him tighter, tears ran in rivers down his own cheeks. Slowly the revelation of emancipation became apparent to the prisoner.

Amrach continued from one to another. It was as if sunlight had already flooded the place. He went from slave to slave and, as he was doing so, he heard the whisper of the Paraclete:

'Remember, Amrach – at the point when your words, however powerful and truthful, fail to reach them, your love always will. When the Chief Prince of Harag fell foaming from his horse they were legally emancipated. But that was not enough, was it?'

'No,' replied Amrach through his tears.

'You see, to be really free they needed to be liberated from within, and your love made that possible. You could have reached them with the truth and left them there. But to really bring them out of the darkness of this prison, it was necessary that they be released from a dungeon even darker that the one they presently inhabit.'

Amrach had now almost reached the end of the line of prisoners and then, for an instant because of the oppressive heat, he removed his helmet to wipe his brow. There were only two slaves yet to be freed and they recognized him only the briefest moment before he recognized them.

His sons! His own boys, still alive!

They flung themselves at him. With one in each arm he hugged them closely to him. And then he led the people out into the warm and welcoming sunshine.

'This is the happiest day in all my life,' said Amrach as he talked again with the Paraclete. 'Where next am I to travel? Where next to pass on this great news?'

'Your next destination is the Stronghold,' said the Paraclete.

'But what of others who need yet to hear? There must be many more in slavery and others that are bound?'

'There are many more and each must, and will, be told – but it is not you who are to tell them.'

'Then how will that come about if I return?' said Amrach.

'Those who have been set free must first both rest and eat. When that is done you must give them a clear account of everything that has taken place. Tell them of everything that has transpired since you first left this land to journey to the land of Phos. Leave out nothing of importance, and let them ask you questions. It is most important that they understand you fully. When you are satisfied that they are clear on all points, and believe that they are physically strong enough to travel, send them out across the land until the message is proclaimed to all.'

'But they have neither armour nor sword.'

'They need neither now,' responded the Paraclete. 'The power that Harag once had is now completely gone. The Lion's name is all they need. No one will be able to stand against them. You and your sons can now return to the Stronghold of Theotes. The whole fortress is bathed in great rejoicing. This is not a celebration you want to miss. You have played a loyal part in this great triumph. Go in strength, faithful Amrach.'

'Faithful Amrach!' These were the words that he had always longed to hear. It was not the power that he had wielded in the Lion's name, nor the exploits that he had accomplished throughout the land of Phos – nothing meant as much as to be called 'faithful'.

In his weakness he had doubted that he would ever make it. It was the Paraclete that had made it possible. The Paraclete had been faithful to him; now he was being called 'faithful', too.

Though their father had told them of the splendour of the Stronghold, nothing had really prepared his sons for seeing it for themselves. They had now recovered well and, as the Watchmen on the walls had informed those in the fortress of their arrival, Aspasmos was there to greet them as they drew near to the approach road.

'The Lion is in the Great Hall. He has been informed of your return. He awaits you all.'

'These are your sons, are they not?' said the Lion as the three of them stood before the throne.

'They are, Sire, and we are together once more because of the great grace bestowed upon us by the Council of Theotes. I have no vocabulary that can adequately express my gratitude, your Majesty. I owe you all I have and more beside. What can I say?'

'You have served well and been faithful, Amrach,' continued the Lion. 'You have carried the Silver Sceptre twice and never once released it from your grasp. Zohah, I know is glad he met you and Entimos and Kalon rejoice that you crossed their path. Darak has become your firmest friend and many others are here today because of your willingness to bear my name throughout the land. They are present to greet you and you will be united with them a little later.'

'Sire, I can see the ones that you have mentioned and others too,' said Amrach, nodding and smiling in recognition as his eyes met the comrades that had been mentioned. 'I can see them all, Sire, except Darak. I trust that all is well with him?'

'Darak indeed is well,' said the Lion. 'My stewards will call him forth. There is someone with him though that I would like you to meet.'

A long crimson curtain next to the throne stirred and, through it, walked Darak with a woman.

'Amrach!' she cried, running to her husband's side.

Gathering their sons into their embrace they watched as the curtain opened yet again. All who had cherished the Remnant Legend streamed forward. Not one of those who had been slain was missing.

'Did I not tell you', said the Lion, 'that there is no such thing as death for those who tread the Lion's path?'

There was much tumultuous rejoicing in the Great Hall that day. It almost drowned out the fanfare of trumpets which gave the orchestras and choirs their introduction, as with great voice, all assembled sang:

> Hail to the Lion, Mighty King
> And Victor over all his foes!
> From sea to sea his people come
> To give him praise and to adore.
> What tongue can tell or lips recite
> The Greatness of his name?
> From coast to coast the nations tell
> His splendour and his fame!

Appendix

Amrach and the Paraclete is an allegory or picture that shows the relationship between God and those he loves. The first thing that the reader notices is that the Lion represents Jesus in the story in the same way that the Paraclete has a parallel with the Holy Spirit. Some people think that the Holy Spirit is just a 'force' or 'power', but the Bible clearly teaches that the Holy Spirit is the third person of the Trinity – represented in the book by 'The Council of Theotes.'

Within the story of Amrach are many spiritual principles that are to be found within the Bible. If you are really adventurous you may want to seek out the elements hidden in the story. To help you, the pages that follow contain Scripture references. Look them up and see if you can discover the part of Amrach's story to which they refer.

Chapter 2

Luke 9:62: 'Jesus replied, "No one who puts his hand to the plough and looks back is fit for service in the kingdom of God."'

Chapter 3

John 14:26-7: 'But the Counsellor, the Holy Spirit, whom the Father will send in my name, will teach you all things and will remind you of everything I have said to you. Peace I leave with you; my peace I give you. I do not give to you as the world gives. Do not let your hearts be troubled and do not be afraid.'

John 16:12-15: 'But when he, the Spirit of truth, comes, he will guide you into all truth. He will not speak on his own; he will speak only what he hears, and he will tell you what is yet to come. He will bring glory to me by taking from what is mine and making it known to you. All that belongs to the Father is mine. That is why I said the Spirit will take from what is mine and make it known to you.'

Jeremiah 1:5-8: '"Before I formed you in the womb I knew you, before you were born I set you apart; I appointed you as a prophet to the nations." "Ah, Sovereign LORD," I said, "I do not know how to speak; I am only a child." But the LORD said to me, "Do not say, 'I am only a child.' You must go to everyone I send you to and say whatever I command you. Do not be afraid of them, for I am with you and will rescue you," declares the LORD.'

Matthew 28:18-20: 'Then Jesus came to them and said, "All authority in heaven and on earth has been given to me. Therefore go and make disciples of all nations, baptising them in the name of the Father and of the Son and of the Holy Spirit, and teaching them to obey everything I have commanded you. And surely I am with you always, to the very end of the age."'

Proverbs 3:5-6: 'Trust in the LORD with all your heart and lean not on your own understanding; in all your ways acknowledge him, and he will make your paths straight.'

Psalms 119:105: 'Your word is a lamp to my feet and a light for my path.'

John 14:12: 'I tell you the truth, anyone who has faith in me will do what I have been doing. He will do even greater things than these, because I am going to the Father.'

Romans 8:11: 'And if the Spirit of him who raised Jesus from the dead is living in you, he who raised Christ from the dead will also give life to your mortal bodies through his Spirit, who lives in you.'

Romans 12:12-13: 'Share with God's people who are in need. Practice hospitality.'

1 Peter 4:8-9: 'Offer hospitality to one another without grumbling.'

Chapter 4

Philippians 4:18-19: 'And my God will meet all your needs according to his glorious riches in Christ Jesus.'

Luke 6:38: 'Give, and it will be given to you. A good measure, pressed down, shaken together and running over, will be poured into your lap. For with the measure you use, it will be measured to you.'

Chapter 5

John 4:23-4: 'Yet a time is coming and has now come when the true worshippers will worship the Father in spirit and truth, for they are the kind of worshippers the Father seeks. God is spirit, and his worshippers must worship in spirit and in truth.'

Chapter 6

Zechariah 4:6: 'So he said to me, "This is the word of the LORD to Zerubbabel: 'Not by might nor by power, but by my Spirit,' says the LORD Almighty."'

Isaiah 53:3: 'He was despised and rejected by men, a man of sorrows, and familiar with suffering. Like one from whom men hide their faces he was despised, and we esteemed him not.'

Ezekiel 3:18-19: 'When I say to a wicked man, "You will surely die," and you do not warn him or speak out to dissuade him from his evil ways in order to save his life, that wicked man will die for his sin, and I will hold you accountable for his blood. But if you do warn the wicked man and he does not turn from his wickedness or from his evil ways, he will die for his sin; but you will have saved yourself.'

Psalms 139:23-4: 'Search me, O God, and know my heart; test me and know my anxious thoughts. See if there is any offensive way in me, and lead me in the way everlasting.'

Matthew 26:33-4: 'Peter replied, "Even if all fall away on account of you, I never will." "I tell you the truth," Jesus answered, "this very night, before the cock crows, you will disown me three times."'

Ephesians 4:30: 'And do not grieve the Holy Spirit of God, with whom you were sealed for the day of redemption.'

Chapter 7

Jeremiah 29:11-13: 'Then you will call upon me and come and pray to me, and I will listen to you. You will seek me and find me when you seek me with all your heart.'

Matthew 23:24: 'You blind guides! You strain out a gnat but swallow a camel.'

Matthew 7:3-5: 'Why do you look at the speck of sawdust in your brother's eye and pay no attention to the plank in your own eye? How can you say to your brother, "Let me take the speck out of your eye," when all the time there is a plank in your own eye? You hypocrite, first take the plank out of your own eye, and then you will see clearly to remove the speck from your brother's eye.'

Mark 7:6-9: 'He replied, "Isaiah was right when he prophesied about you hypocrites; as it is written: 'These people honour me with their lips, but their hearts are far from me. They worship me in vain; their teachings are but rules taught by men.' You have let go of the commands of God and are holding on to the traditions of men." And he said to them: "You have a fine way of setting aside the commands of God in order to observe your own traditions!"'

Matthew 10:34: 'Do not suppose that I have come to bring peace to the earth. I did not come to bring peace, but a sword.'

John 2:25: 'He did not need man's testimony about man, for he knew what was in a man.'

Chapter 8

Isaiah 55:8-9: 'For my thoughts are not your thoughts, neither are your ways my ways,' declares the LORD. 'As the heavens are higher than the earth, so are my ways higher than your ways and my thoughts than your thoughts.'

1 John 1:8-9: 'If we claim to be without sin, we deceive ourselves and the truth is not in us. If we confess our sins, he is faithful and just and will forgive us our sins and purify us from all unrighteousness.'

2 Corinthians 5:20-21: 'God made him who had no sin to be sin for us, so that in him we might become the righteousness of God.'

1 Corinthians 15:3-4: 'For what I received I passed on to you as of first importance: that Christ died for our sins according to the Scriptures, that he was buried, that he was raised on the third day according to the Scriptures.'

1 Peter 3:17-19: 'For Christ died for sins once for all, the righteous for the unrighteous, to bring you to God. He

was put to death in the body but made alive by the Spirit.'

John 3:16-18: 'For God so loved the world that he gave his one and only Son, that whoever believes in him shall not perish but have eternal life. For God did not send his Son into the world to condemn the world, but to save the world through him.'

John 1:10-13: 'He was in the world, and though the world was made through him, the world did not recognise him. He came to that which was his own, but his own did not receive him. Yet to all who received him, to those who believed in his name, he gave the right to become children of God – children born not of natural descent, nor of human decision or a husband's will, but born of God.'

Hebrews 9:27-8: 'Just as man is destined to die once, and after that to face judgment, so Christ was sacrificed once to take away the sins of many people; and he will appear a second time, not to bear sin, but to bring salvation to those who are waiting for him.'

1 Corinthians 15:22-3: 'For as in Adam all die, so in Christ all will be made alive.'

Luke 5:8: 'When Simon Peter saw this, he fell at Jesus' knees and said, "Go away from me, Lord; I am a sinful man!"'

Chapter 9

Hebrews 11:1: 'Now faith is being sure of what we hope for and certain of what we do not see.'

1 John 5:14-15: 'This is the confidence we have in approaching God: that if we ask anything according to his will, he hears us. And if we know that he hears us – whatever we ask-we know that we have what we asked of him.'

Exodus 17:12: 'When Moses' hands grew tired, they took a stone and put it under him and he sat on it. Aaron and Hur held his hands up – one on one side, one on the other – so that his hands remained steady till sunset.'

John 3:14-15: 'Just as Moses lifted up the snake in the desert, so the Son of Man must be lifted up, that everyone who believes in him may have eternal life.'

Chapter 10

Galatians 3:26-9: 'You are all sons of God through faith in Christ Jesus, for all of you who were baptised into Christ have clothed yourselves with Christ. There is neither Jew nor Greek, slave nor free, male nor female, for you are all one in Christ Jesus.'

Luke 15:3-7: 'Then Jesus told them this parable: "Suppose one of you has a hundred sheep and loses one of them. Does he not leave the ninety-nine in the open country and go after the lost sheep until he finds it? And when he finds it, he joyfully puts it on his shoulders and goes home. Then he calls his friends and neighbours together and says, 'Rejoice with me; I have found my lost sheep.' I tell you that in the same way there will be more rejoicing in heaven over one sinner who repents than over ninety-nine righteous persons who do not need to repent."'

Chapter 11

Jeremiah 1:4-5: 'The word of the LORD came to me, saying, "Before I formed you in the womb I knew you, before you were born I set you apart; I appointed you as a prophet to the nations."'

Romans 6:23: 'For the wages of sin is death, but the gift of God is eternal life in Christ Jesus our Lord.'

Chapter 12

Romans 8:31: 'What, then, shall we say in response to this? If God is for us, who can be against us?'

Psalms 16:11: 'You have made known to me the path of life; you will fill me with joy in your presence, with eternal pleasures at your right hand.'

John 15:11: 'I have told you this so that my joy may be in you and that your joy may be complete.'

Chapter 13

Hebrews 4:16: 'Let us then approach the throne of grace with confidence, so that we may receive mercy and find grace to help us in our time of need.'

Isaiah 55:11: 'So is my word that goes out from my mouth: It will not return to me empty, but will accomplish what I desire and achieve the purpose for which I sent it.'

Chapter 14

Ephesians 6:10-18: 'Finally, be strong in the Lord and in his mighty power. Put on the full armour of God so that you can take your stand against the devil's schemes. For our struggle is not against flesh and blood, but against the rulers, against the authorities, against the powers of this dark world and against the spiritual forces of evil in the heavenly realms. Therefore put on the full armour of God, so that when the day of evil comes, you may be able to stand your ground, and after you have done everything, to stand. Stand firm then, with the belt of truth buckled around your waist, with the breastplate of righteousness in place, and with your feet fitted with the readiness that comes from the gospel of peace. In addition to all this, take up the shield of faith, with which you can extinguish all the flaming arrows of the evil one. Take the helmet of salvation and the sword of the Spirit, which is the word of God. And pray in the Spirit on all occasions with all kinds of prayers and requests. With this in mind, be alert and always keep on praying for all the saints.'

Hebrews 4:12-13: 'For the word of God is living and active. Sharper than any double-edged sword, it penetrates even to dividing soul and spirit, joints and marrow; it judges the thoughts and attitudes of the heart. Nothing in all creation is hidden from God's sight. Everything is uncovered and laid bare before the eyes of him to whom we must give account.'

Isaiah 14:12-15: 'How you have fallen from heaven, O morning star, son of the dawn! You have been cast down to the earth, you who once laid low the nations! You said in your heart, "I will ascend to heaven; I will raise my throne above the stars of God; I will sit enthroned on the mount of assembly, on the utmost heights of the sacred mountain. I will ascend above the tops of the clouds; I will make myself like the Most High." But you are brought down to the grave, to the depths of the pit.'

John 6:47: 'I tell you the truth, he who believes has everlasting life.'

Daniel 12:2: 'Multitudes who sleep in the dust of the earth will awake: some to everlasting life, others to shame and everlasting contempt.'

Matthew 25:46: 'Then they will go away to eternal punishment, but the righteous to eternal life.'

John 15:16-17: 'You did not choose me, but I chose you and appointed you to go and bear fruit – fruit that will last. Then the Father will give you whatever you ask in my name. This is my command: Love each other.'

Chapter 15

2 Timothy 1:10b: '. . . Christ Jesus, who has destroyed death and has brought life and immortality to light through the gospel.'

1 John 3:8b: 'The reason the Son of God appeared was to destroy the devil's work.'

John 5:21-3: 'The Father judges no one, but has entrusted all judgment to the Son, that all may honour the Son just as they honour the Father. He who does not honour the Son does not honour the Father, who sent him.'

Chapter 16

James 2:26: 'As the body without the spirit is dead, so faith without deeds is dead.'

1 John 3:16: 'This is how we know what love is: Jesus Christ laid down his life for us. And we ought to lay down our lives for our brothers.'

Isaiah 54:17: '"No weapon forged against you will prevail, and you will refute every tongue that accuses you. This is the heritage of the servants of the LORD, and this is their vindication from me," declares the LORD.'

John 8:36: 'If the Son sets you free, you will be free indeed.'

Matt 25:21: 'His master replied, "Well done, good and faithful servant! You have been faithful with a few things; I will put you in charge of many things. Come and share your master's happiness!"'